HATCHET HOLLOW

A BLACK ROSE MYSTERY, BOOK 2

AMANDA MCKINNEY

HH TISEVICH

Paperback ISBN
eBook ISBN 978-0-9995553-3-0
Paperback ISBN 978-0-999553-2-3

https://www.amandamckinneyauthor.com

DEDICATION

For Mama.

ALSO BY AMANDA

THRILLER NOVELS:

The Sketch Artist

The Perfect Murder

The Stranger in My Bed

A Marriage of Lies

When I Disappear

The Wife's Silence

The Widow of Weeping Pines: A Thriller Novella

The Raven's Wife: A Thriller Novella

The Lie Between Us: A Thriller Novella

ROMANTIC THRILLER NOVELS:

THE ANTI-HERO:

Mine

BESTSELLING STEELE SHADOWS SERIES:

Cabin 1 (Steele Shadows Security)

Cabin 2 (Steele Shadows Security)

Cabin 3 (Steele Shadows Security)

Phoenix (Steele Shadows Rising)

Jagger (Steele Shadows Investigations)

Ryder (Steele Shadows Investigations)

Her Mercenary (Steele Shadows Mercenaries)

Her Renegade (Steele Shadows Mercenaries)

ON THE EDGE SERIES:

Buried Deception

Trail of Deception

THE BERRY SPRINGS SERIES:

The Woods (A Berry Springs Novel)

The Lake (A Berry Springs Novel)

The Storm (A Berry Springs Novel)

The Fog (A Berry Springs Novel)

The Creek (A Berry Springs Novel)

The Shadow (A Berry Springs Novel)

The Cave (A Berry Springs Novel)

THE ROAD SERIES:

Rattlesnake Road

Redemption Road

The Viper

Devil's Gold (A Black Rose Mystery, Book 1)

Hatchet Hollow (A Black Rose Mystery, Book 2)

Tomb's Tale (A Black Rose Mystery Book 3)

Evil Eye (A Black Rose Mystery Book 4)

Sinister Secrets (A Black Rose Mystery Book 5)

And many more to come...

LET'S CONNECT!

Get early access, exclusive deals, and a behind-the-scenes look at Amanda's world.

Join Amanda's newsletter for new releases, limited-time promos, personal notes, and the stories behind the stories— sent straight to your inbox.

https://www.amandamckinneyauthor.com/contact

HATCHET HOLLOW

After an afternoon of mind-numbingly boring surveillance in the woods, Private Investigator Raven Cane goes for a twilight jog to clear her head, only to discover a gruesome murder in the town's most notorious cave, Hatchet Hollow. Minutes later, the impossibly handsome Lieutenant Zander Stone arrives at the scene to take over, but Raven has a hard time letting the case go. Why did the killer cut off the victim's fingers? More importantly, who would do such a thing?

After a failed attempt at tracking down the elusive Marden Balik, aka, the legendary witch of the Great Shadow Mountains, Zander dives headfirst into Devil's Den's most recent murder, only to uncover twists and turns at every step— including a secret book of curses that may, or may not, exist. As the list of suspects grows, Zander does his best to keep Raven at arm's length. But Raven is persistent, nosing her way into his case, making it increasingly difficult to keep his concentration on the task at hand, and off of her sultry body.

And when another woman is found brutally murdered, Zander worries that Raven has gotten too close to the investigation... close enough to put her directly in the killer's sights.

PROLOGUE

$\mathcal{A}$ BLACK CROW swooped down from a decaying pine tree beside her, its cringing caw piercing the silence of the woods. She shuddered and zipped up her windbreaker.

Abby never liked crows, or birds for that matter. Not since her parents brought her back a rare, *extremely expensive*—their words, not hers—parrot from Honduras when she was twelve years old. It was one of the many vacations they'd taken without her—needing a break, they'd say—and leaving her with her nanny, Fran, whose hair always looked, ironically, like a bird's nest. And whose breath could stop a clock. The same nanny who'd tattled on her for leaving a window open, allowing the precious parrot to fly away.

Her father didn't speak to her for a week, and her mother, only when he wasn't looking.

But that was a long time ago. That was then, and this was now. She was a woman now, freshly turned twenty-one with her whole life ahead of her. She didn't need her parents or the shallow gifts they'd showered her with, replacing their inability to show affection. She didn't need them anymore, just like they didn't need her. That's how they always made her feel, anyway.

A cool gust of wind carrying the sour scent of moldy earth swept past her. She glanced up at the cloud-covered sky. Another dreary day. Another stupid, dull day in this small, suffocating, godforsaken town—just like the day before.

But not anymore.

She could make her own decisions now, out from under their financial thumb. Go her own way in life.

And she was.

And her parents would kill her for it.

Abby stepped onto the jogging trail that snaked through the woods and stumbled on a rock. Dammit, she was a mess. She looked down at her new *black* running shoes laced tightly over *black* ankle socks. *Black* leggings and a *black* T-shirt.

Black.

She swallowed the lump in her throat and took off down the trail.

Abby had always been fascinated with the mystical, creepy folktales that were whispered through the Great Shadow Mountains. Spirits, ghosts... witches. Hundreds of stories told during dark nights with no electricity, bonfires with too many drinks, Halloween, or just about any scenario shrouded in darkness. The stories were told with glances over the shoulder and hushed voices laced with fear, and if you listened carefully enough, respect. Respect for the evil forces that could snatch you up in the middle of the night, turn you into a lizard, or worse, curse you and everyone you loved.

Witches who could raise the dead from the earth.

Witches who could take your life.

Respect, power. Those were the two things Abby was promised when she'd been approached about "turning over a new leaf". Taking control of her own life—and others if needed. Yes, she would be a part of something now, of something big, she was told.

Abby took a deep breath.

Was she apprehensive? Absolutely. But what they'd promised her had been too great to ignore. She'd have been a fool to walk away.

Right?

She smoothed her black windbreaker.

Black really wasn't her color, but they had been wearing it—head-to-toe—so she figured she'd better get used to it. There would be so much to learn, they'd explained, and embracing black was a good start, she guessed.

But dammit, it *really* washed her out. Abby's pale complexion and light blonde hair—a gift from her mother —looked even more lifeless against the unforgiving color.

Maybe she would take baby steps into the change.

Yes, baby steps.

Maybe it would be okay if she wore her red silk blouse and white Louboutin six-inch heels on her date next week.

Butterflies tickled her stomach.

A date!

She couldn't believe it. Yes, *she* had been asked out by a good-looking, accomplished man, nonetheless. It was completely out of left field... and only hours after she'd officially committed to "turning over a new leaf." Coincidence?

Yes, things were going to change for her. Things were going to go her way, for the first freaking time in her life.

She was going to be powerful, respected. Feared.

With an extra pep in her step, Abby rounded a corner in

the trail and spotted her new jogging partner anxiously waiting ahead.

"Hey."

"Hey, there. You ready?"

Abby snorted. "As ready as I can be, I guess."

"First mile's always the hardest. I'll take it easy on you. Might want to stick those keys in your pocket, though. Uneven terrain."

"Oh, okay. Yeah." She nodded, looked down, and as she unzipped her pocket—

WHACK!

Her head snapped back as a fist slammed into her jaw.

Pain rocketed through her skull. Bright lights flashed in her eyes. The metallic taste of blood filled her mouth as she stumbled backward. The world spun around her, sending a wave of nausea through her body as she tried to process what was happening.

What the *hell*?

She opened her eyes to fuzziness and tried to focus on the movement in front of her. But before she could come to, the next brutal force knocked her out cold.

1

OMINOUS, GREY CLOUDS drifted over the setting sun, casting darkness over the Great Shadow Mountains.

"Well, *shit.*" Zander looked over at Hunter in the driver's seat, as he dipped the helicopter lower, soaring just above the pine trees below.

"Well, shit is right. Can barely see now."

"Spring storms coming early this year."

Hunter hesitated a moment before saying, "We're going to have to call this thing off soon, you know. It's been, what? A few weeks now?"

Zander clenched his jaw. There were two things Lieutenant Zander Stone were known for—making women fall to their knees, and his inability to drop a case. Ever.

It had been over two weeks since he'd arrested Marden Balik for holding her sister, Agnes, captive for forty years, for having an affair with her husband. Two weeks since Balik mysteriously escaped her jail cell and burned the letter *K* into the guard's forehead. Two weeks of rampant small-town rumors that Marden Balik was actually Krestel, the rumored witch of the Great Shadow Mountains.

Frustrated, Zander raised the binoculars and scanned the vast forest below. "Where the *hell* did she go?"

Hunter shook his head. "Needle in a haystack, man. Needle in a haystack. And we're only assuming she hid somewhere in the mountains, right?"

"Right. According to her sister, Balik spent most of her time in the woods."

"Doing what, exactly?"

Zander cleared his throat. "Meeting with her *coven*, she thinks, but that's only an assumption. Agnes wasn't exactly willing to spend ample time with us when we interviewed her."

"I don't blame her. If my sister had kept me chained inside a house for forty years, doing God knows what, I'd want to get the hell out of dodge, too. Where'd she go?"

"Booked the first flight out to Ireland, to stay with some distant relatives. I doubt she'll ever return to the States." He blew out a breath. "How the hell did Balik break out of that damn jail cell?" He shook his head, gazing out at the mountains. "She's got to be here somewhere. Close."

"No trace of her whatsoever, right? Credit cards, cell phone, nothing?"

"Nothing. Zip. Nada. It's like she disappeared into thin air. Or these damn mountains, which have endless places to hide."

A moment ticked by as they surveyed the woods.

"Maybe she turned herself into a coyote, or snake, or a two-headed horse, or something."

Zander lowered the binoculars and rolled his eyes. "You really think she's a witch, Hunter?"

Hunter shrugged as the helicopter skimmed dangerously close to the peak of a mountain. "The legend of Krestel goes back decades... hell, I remember my granddad telling me stories about her on Halloween night. Remember old man Stevens? And how his fifty head of cattle mysteriously died one night, not twenty-four hours after he created a petition to outlaw any so-called witches, or practice of witchcraft, here in Devil's Den? He had to file bankruptcy. His wife left him. It ruined his life. And remember Mary Lou? Went deaf and blind after claiming she saw Krestel raise demons from the earth one night in the woods."

Zander cut him the side-eye.

"Okay, just one more—although I could go on and on. Remember Cindy Hampstead? Orphaned after she woke up to every one of her family members dead? Rumor was that her mom was part of Krestel's coven, and wanted out, and threatened to reveal the identities of Krestel's followers. That was Krestel's revenge."

"So you *do* think she's a witch? That she's Krestel? You believe it?"

Pause. "I learned a long time ago that sometimes things aren't as they appear."

Zander nodded. As a former military intelligence officer, Caleb Hunter had been on the receiving end of plenty of surprises over the course of his career.

Hunter continued, "What exactly did you dig up on her?"

"Marden Balik was born and raised here in Devil's Den, nothing of interest in her childhood. She worked as the school librarian until she retired a decade ago. No close friends, parents died decades ago, and she kept to herself, mainly. No record, hell, not even a damn speeding ticket. Woman's as clean as a whistle."

"No friends at all?"

"Nope."

Hunter chewed on his lower lip. "Let's assume for a second—

"You know I don't like assumptions, Hunter."

"Humor me then, you narrow-minded tight-ass. As I was saying, let's assume that the rumor *is* true, that Marden Balik is Krestel, the witch of the Great Shadow Mountains. So then, according to the legends, she's the head of a *large* coven of witches."

"According to the legends, yes."

"So... more than one witch. Here in Devil's Den."

Zander met Hunter's gaze, and for a moment, they just stared at each other, letting the disturbing thought sink in.

Just then, a thin trail of ink-black smoke snaked up from a mountaintop in the distance.

Zander scooted to the edge of his seat and peered through his binoculars. "Whoa, you see that? Just beyond the clearing?"

"What am I, blind? Yeah, I see it."

"Any houses out here?"

"Hell no, not for miles and miles."

"That's a lot of smoke for a campfire."

"And black as coal."

A zing of excitement—hopefulness—shot up Zander's spine. Could they have finally found Marden Balik? He shifted in his seat, and craned his neck for a better angle. "Let's check it out."

"You got it, boss." Hunter accelerated, zooming over the mountains.

Zander's pulse picked up as they drew closer. There was something about the way the smoke moved—how it curved and danced in the wind that made his senses pique.

Hunter slowed, hovering just above a small clearing.

Sprinkles of rain began to dot the windshield. Darkness was closing in.

"Looks like it's coming from a few yards in the woods."

"And definitely not a forest fire."

"Want me to land?"

"Yeah, let's check it out on foot before the storm hits."

Suddenly, a bright light shot out from the smoke, piercing through the helicopter windshield.

"Son of a bitch!" Hunter squinted, blocking the beam of light with his hand.

Zander jerked down the binoculars, tears welling in his eyes. "What the *fuck?* What the hell was that?"

Hunter squeezed his eyes shut, and shook his head, swiping at his eyes.

"You okay, man?"

"Yeah, that fucking blinded me for a minute. Spots all over my vision."

Zander looked back at the smoke. "What the *fuck*?"

Hunter wiped his watering eyes with the back of his hand. "Maybe some dumbass teenage punk with one of those laser lights or some shit."

"All the way out here? No way. Land this son of a bitch. Let's check it out."

With a deep breath, Hunter gripped the control stick and began to descend.

Zander's heart started to race as they neared the ground. He squinted and leaned forward. Was that... a small group of people? Standing just beyond the tree line? *No way.* He blinked, refocused the lens. It *was*—and they were standing in a circle, cloaked in black, creepily swaying back and forth. "I, uh... think I see something. People, maybe. Get lower."

"You got it."

As the helicopter lowered, a massive cloud of black

smoke suddenly burst from the woods, engulfing the helicopter.

"*Fuck!*"

"I can't see a Goddamned thing!"

A darkness as black as tar surrounded them.

"Pull back!"

The helicopter tipped and lurched to the side. Zander gripped the seat as his body slammed into the window. His heart hammered as he looked over at Hunter.

"You okay? You got it, man?"

A bead of sweat rolled down Hunter's forehead, as his gaze stayed laser-focused on the controls.

Zander leaned forward. "*Hunter?* You good?"

Just then, the helicopter sputtered, and an eerie silence filled the cab just before it tipped forward and plunged into the darkness.

2

*R*AVEN SQUEEZED HER face and shifted her weight, attempting to roll off the twig that had been poking into her ribcage for the last forty-five minutes.

Snick.

The twig snapped in half, the sound echoing through the woods.

She froze, held her breath, and peered through the long-range camera.

Phew. Eric Stevens hadn't so much as lifted a finger as he sat, alone, on the tailgate of his truck, in a small field just beyond the tree line.

Raven blew out an exhale. That was close. A cool breeze blew her long, brown hair across her face. She took a deep breath, inhaling the crisp mountain air. Although there were stubborn patches of ice still clinging to the valleys from the last winter storm, spring was almost here, and she couldn't wait. She lowered the camera and took a moment to look at the view.

In a leather jacket, black beanie, and black jogging pants, Raven was perched high on one of the many cliffs that made up the Great Shadow Mountains. Dusk sat on the horizon, its bright colors of orange, fuchsia, and red fading into the thick, grey clouds that hung heavily just above her head, it seemed. The sweet scent of rain carried in the wind, a polite reminder of the impending storm, as promised by Stan the Weatherman. Dark shadows stretched across the ground below her, darkening the dense woods that ran for miles and miles.

They weren't called the Great Shadow Mountains for nothing.

In the distance, she heard the low rumble of a helicopter and had no doubt it was Devil's Den PD, still looking for the elusive Marden Balik, aka, Krestel, the legendary witch of the mountains. She shook her head, hoping they would find her, ASAP, which would help to ease the citizens of Devil's Den. The small town had been in a constant state of fear after a recent string of vicious murders, *and* from the realization that a witch had walked among them for decades.

Raven glanced back at the field, and a yawn caught her. She kicked herself for not bringing a thermos of coffee—or wine, or hell, anything with liquor in it—in her bag. It had been a hell of a day, and now, there she was, at seven o'clock in the evening, lying on her stomach over a bed of rocks, surveilling a man suspected of insider trading.

Boooring.

If luck was on her side, and if her intel was correct, Eric would be meeting with the Coleman brothers—one, a state senator, and the other a prominent plastic surgeon—to divulge confidential information about an up-and-coming pharmaceutical company, in exchange for sixty-thousand dollars. Black Rose Investigations had been hired by Eric's firm, who suspected him of insider trading for some time. But it wasn't until Eric hit the Securities Exchange Commission's radar that the firm decided to take action, so they didn't have to take the hit. Raven's boss, Dixie Knight—one of the most sought-after private investigators in the country—had given the case to Raven, much to her surprise. It was her first solo case and the first time for her to prove herself worthy of being promoted from an assistant to an official PI. Raven had been working her ass off, from morning to night, seven days a week, and she was more than ready to take on her own cases, even if they were a total snoozefest, like this one.

She sighed, lifted the camera again.

But really, what else did she have to do? There certainly was no date she had to primp for, or man waiting for her at home—his sexy, muscular body holding a bouquet of flowers in one hand and a glass of champagne in the other. No, the only thing waiting for her at home was a frozen quinoa... something in the freezer, a half-drunk bottle of wine, and a mountain of laundry that gave her anxiety just thinking about it.

Okay, so she had the wine going for her, at least.

Raven reached back, unzipped the front pocket of her bag and yanked out a small plastic baggie of almonds— twelve to be exact. A perfectly healthy snack. She popped a few in her mouth, then carefully placed the baggie back into the designated "snack" pocket, which was in-between her fingerprint kit and recorder pen. It was a bag that she always kept with her, as did every member of the Black Rose Investigations team—their spy-kit as they jokingly called it. Each bag had everything necessary for researching cases and examining crime scenes. Flashlights, magnifying glasses, latex gloves and booties, recorder pens and notebooks. And in the front pocket was the gun that every woman of Black Rose carried with them—a Glock 19 with a hot-pink handle and the letters *BRI* engraved down the side. And true to form, Raven's bag was impeccably organized, labeled, color-coordinated, and spotless.

Just like her life.

Raven Cane was known for three things—her obsessive attention to detail, her tireless commitment to the job, and, above all else, her incessant need for organization. Raven ran on schedules, plans, and to-do lists, and wouldn't have it any other way. She was always prepared for absolutely anything that might come her way.

Neurotic? Maybe. A bit high-strung? Sure. But Raven had convinced herself that her neurosis would make her one hell of a private investigator someday.

Someday.

Her gaze shifted to the Red Rock hiking trail below, and she released a low groan. She'd promised herself that she'd go for a jog after surveillance, even though she'd already completed ninety minutes of hot yoga earlier in the day—right after cleaning her house top to bottom, as she did every Sunday.

Never rest.

Her attention was drawn to a shiny red sports car bouncing down the dirt road in the distance. A spurt of energy shot through her system—the Coleman brothers, perhaps?

Oh, please, please, please be the Coleman brothers.

Her pulse picked up as she grabbed her camera, then shimmied forward on her elbows for a better look.

She zoomed in as the car rolled to a stop next to Eric's truck. The driver's side door opened. Her brow tipped up as a tall, busty blonde slid out, wearing a low-cut sweater, skin-tight pants, and bejeweled cowboy boots. Even at her distance she could see the woman's cleavage. Impressive.

But definitely not the Coleman brothers.

Click, click.

She scanned over to Eric, who smiled and jumped off the tailgate. The woman met him at the bed of the truck, and after a short exchange, Eric unveiled a bouquet of roses that was hidden behind his back.

Raven wrinkled her nose. Lucky bitch.

The woman leapt into his arms and began kissing him wildly.

Eric spun the woman around and heaved her onto the tailgate, pushing himself in-between her legs.

Raven's eyes widened. Um, this definitely was *not* insider trading. Well, of the financial kind, anyway.

The mid-day rendezvous continued as Eric pulled the woman's sweater over her head revealing her bare skin.

Raven felt the heat rising to her cheeks as the sweater was tossed to the ground. She cocked an eyebrow—wow, no bra, now she was *really* impressed. She always wanted to be the type of woman who was confident enough to go without a bra. Woman power! Right? Wrong. Thanks to her barely B-cups, Raven not only opted for a bra every day, she wore one that had about an inch of padding. It wasn't like anyone had been trying to grab them—and uncover her padded secret—lately, anyway.

Raven watched Eric kiss the lucky woman's breasts, spending ample time on each nipple.

It had been so long since she'd had a man spend ample time on any part of her body.

She cleared her throat, shook her head. *Dammit, get a hold of yourself, pervo.* She was here for work, for Christ's sake. And her job was to take pictures of whoever Eric was meeting in the woods, and by God, she was going to do just that.

She squared her shoulders, ignoring the sweat that was starting to bead under her shirt, and reminded herself that she was a professional, and *not* a pervert. Even though it had been more than a year since she'd had sex. Okay, two.

She zoomed in just as Eric slowly slid down the woman's pants... followed by her leopard-print panties.

Raven's eyes bugged. Her heart began to race.

Oh, my God, oh, my God, oh, my God.

The woman spread her legs and—

She dropped the camera.

Okey-dokey, time to pack up.

As Raven started to push herself up from the ground, she glanced out of the corner of her eye, trying to make out the blurry interaction between Eric and the woman, in the distance. It was like a car accident—she couldn't look away.

Maybe just one more look—to make sure the Coleman brothers hadn't pulled up. Yeah, one more look.

She held up the camera again.

Her mouth gaped as she saw Eric's head slowly slide from side-to-side between the woman's legs, with her hands firmly on the top of his head.

Oh. My. God.

And then, as if her finger had a mind of its own—*click, click, click.*

The woman gripped the side of the truck and arched her back like a sexy feline. Eric's fingers joined his mouth between her legs and then...

She yanked down the camera.

What the hell are you doing? You sick, sick woman! Delete the pictures!

Just then, a scream vibrated through the air. She jerked up the camera again to see the woman laid out on the tailgate, with a satisfied smile on her face.

Raven sighed, shook her head and began packing up. She needed a freaking boyfriend. *Immediately.* That, or she needed to take a quick trip to the adult store downtown on her way home.

After making—sulking was more like it—her way down the mountain, she pulled her cell phone from her pocket and clicked it on.

"Dixie here."

It was seven-thirty Sunday evening and Raven's boss was in the office, working on one of the million cases she had going.

"Hey, it's Raven."

"Did you get it? The pictures?"

She cleared her throat. "Uh, yeah I got some pictures…"

"Of Eric meeting the Coleman brothers? Did you get a picture of them exchanging money, like, a shot of the actual money? Because that's what we need."

"Well… Eric was definitely trading something, that's for sure. He met a blonde, and uh, let's just say she's leaving a very satisfied customer, but not from learning which stocks are about to hit."

"Soooo no meeting with the brothers?"

"No."

Pause. "So… he just banged some chick in the woods? That's it?"

"Appears that way."

Another pause. "I'm not going to ask how long you watched them, Rave. You sick, sick, woman."

"I didn't see the finale, and let's just leave it at that."

A chuckle sounded from the other end of the phone. "Okay, so do we know the lucky woman?"

"Nope, but I'll give the camera to Ace, and have him run a facial recognition scan."

"Sounds good. Let's get that done ASAP. And Rave? You really need to get a boyfriend."

She rolled her eyes. "See you tomorrow, boss."

"See ya."

Click.

3

———

*R*aven unlocked her car and glanced up at the darkening sky. Thick clouds had moved in, absorbing the last of the day's sun and leaving a dim grey light that would soon fade into night. She estimated she had about an hour before it turned completely dark—just enough time to fulfill her promise to herself for a quick jog on the trail.

She placed her camera into its case, taking the time to roll the neck strap into a perfect, tight circle. After securing her bag in the back, she pulled off her leather jacket, folding it into a square on the backseat. Raven grabbed her pocket knife from the console, and slid her keys and cell phone into her pocket. Check, check, check.

The red sports car came flying down the dirt road. The busty, blonde woman zoomed by with a smile plastered on her face.

She rolled her eyes—*lucky, lucky bitch*.

Raven stretched her arms over her head and looked around. Other than a vacant blue pickup truck and red sedan, she was the only person in the gravel parking lot, which wasn't surprising considering the impending rain.

She stretched her neck from side-to-side.

Okay, it's go-time.

Raven stepped onto the trail and took off in a light jog. While most people exercised with headphones in, listening to their favorite mix of *let's get pumped up* music, Raven preferred to listen to the sounds of nature around her. That, and she knew how important it was to always be aware of your surroundings, no matter what. Blame the job.

A mile in, her legs began to loosen, her head began to clear, and the endorphins began to kick in, giving her a much-needed runner's high. The smell of rain became stronger as the woods began to darken.

Up ahead, she spied another jogger in a baseball cap and dark sunglasses. She nodded as they passed. He was tall, built, and cute, and she fought the urge to turn around to check out his backside.

Damn, it had been a long time since she'd had her hands on someone's backside.

Officially sexually frustrated, she pushed into a sprint, inhaling and exhaling the fresh, mountain air. Tingles broke out over her skin as she seemed to fly across the trail. Her thoughts faded from work, and all the cases she had going on, to the laundry waiting for her at home, and then back to the hot jogger she'd just passed.

Okay, maybe everyone was right, she needed a damn boyfriend.

Her heart thrummed as she rounded a corner, stumbling on loose rocks. A chill suddenly ran up her spine. Her senses piqued.

She slowed, noticing a flock of buzzards flying in circles above the trees.

Buzzards.

She looked into the dense woods, focusing on a large rock formation in the distance, where the birds aggressively swooped down, then back up.

Hatchet Hollow.

Hatchet Hollow was a small cave located just a few yards from Red Rock Trail. With an entrance barely wide enough to fit through, the cave was widely avoided, thanks to the haunted rumors that surrounded it.

She'd never set foot in it.

Raven stopped and gazed into the woods.

Probably just a dead squirrel or something. But it was *a lot* of buzzards.

She glanced up and down the trail, contemplating.

And then, as if being pulled like a magnet, she stepped off the trail and into the woods.

The breeze halted. The birds seemed to stop singing as she walked through the thick brush.

She glanced over her shoulder and then pulled out her pocket knife—better safe than sorry. With her eyes locked on the rock in the distance, she flicked up the blade, nicking her finger in the process. Pain zinged through her hand, and she kicked herself for being distracted. She wiped the blood on her pants and pressed on until she finally stepped onto the large rock.

The hair on the back of her neck stood up.

A million flies buzzed overhead, zipping in and out of the narrow opening of the cave, which was almost completely hidden by deep crevasses.

Raven took another glance over her shoulder, then carefully stepped down the slick, moss-covered rocks. She gripped her knife as she neared the cave entrance—pitch-black inside.

As she stood staring into the cave, she thought of all the horror movies she'd seen where the damsel in distress always made the dumbest decisions, most notably, going into a dark house, alone, investigating an ominous noise or something.

She wrinkled her nose—*don't be stupid, Raven.*

She should go back.

She started to turn, but then turned back, and decided to follow her gut that was screaming at her to go into the cave.

With her knife in one hand, and phone glowing in the other, she stepped inside. The smell hit her like a punch in the face.

"Oh, *God*," she whispered as she covered her nose with the back of her hand.

Her heart started to pound, her legs trembled as she forced herself forward, shining the light on the walls.

An eerie silence filled the cave, with only the *drip, drip, drip* from the stalactites echoing through the air.

She took another step and slipped on a slick rock. Stumbling to catch herself, the knife and cell phone flew from her hands and tumbled to the ground, illuminating the corner of the cave.

She gasped.

Just beyond a dip in the cave floor, lay a body of a young woman, pale and motionless.

Raven crossed the cave in two swift steps and gaped down at the body.

The woman's bloodshot eyes grotesquely protruded from her skull, staring blankly at the dark cave ceiling. A thin trickle of dried blood ran from the corner of her blue lips, down her neck. And as Raven's gaze moved down the body, her stomach sank to her feet. The woman's fingers had been cut off—every single one of them.

"Oh, my God."

Bile rose in her throat as she looked at the bloody nubs at the end of the woman's hands.

Oh my God, oh my God, oh my God.

Her stomach churned, and for a moment, she thought she was going to vomit.

Don't throw up on a crime scene, you'll destroy potential evidence, you idiot!

Raven inhaled, swallowed the saliva that had gathered in her mouth, and forced herself to get a grip—get in control of the situation. Her shock slowly began to fade, and the cool-headed, calm, laser-focused demeanor that she was known for began to settle in.

She squatted down for a closer look.

The woman's skin was pale, almost ghostly white. Her muscles were frozen in full rigor mortis. She assumed she'd been deceased for twenty-four hours, tops. Purple bruising speckled her jawline, running across her skinny neck.

Raven shook her head, stood, and grabbed her cell phone from the ground. No reception in the cave, of course, so she jogged outside and dialed 911.

As Raven gave the dispatcher the details and her location, her eyes scanned the ground for any obvious evidence but saw none. The dispatcher promised someone was on their way, and she clicked off the phone.

She glanced up at the sky, now blanketed by storm clouds. Nightfall was coming. The woods would be completely dark in less than thirty minutes.

A cool breeze rustled the leaves above. A buzzard called out. She looked around—acutely aware of the fact that she was completely alone. Just her and a dead body. Alone, in the middle of woods that stretched as far as she could see—so many places to run, to hide.

Who had done this?

4

*V*OICES ECHOING IN the distance had Raven turning on her heel. A flashlight bounced off the trees. The light was running out, quickly.

An officer stepped through the trees. "Miss Cane?"

"Hey, Deena." She blew out a breath of relief. "And *good Lord*, call me Raven."

Officer Deena Malone, the newest member of the police force, had spent her career working security for the state capitol building before moving to Devil's Den. In her mid-forties with bleach-blonde hair, Deena was a beer-drinking, gun-toting Southern cowgirl who spent her spare time running a security equipment side-business out of her garage. She was the most masculine woman Raven had ever met, with the attitude to match.

"You're lucky I didn't call you something else—I'd just curled up with a Bloody Mary and a new horror book."

"And you wonder why you're still single."

Deena grinned. "Ain't that callin' the kettle black." She looked past her. "In the cave?"

Raven nodded.

"Let me go take a look. I'll be right back."

As Deena stepped off the rock, she heard someone else behind her. She turned, and her stomach dropped to her feet. Wearing jeans, a black T-shirt, and a worn leather jacket, the impossibly handsome Lieutenant Zander Stone stepped briskly through the brush... the impossibly handsome Lieutenant that she'd had a crush on since the first time she laid eyes on him when she moved to town, two years ago.

A cell phone was pressed to his ear, and his deep voice carried through the wind, strong, with authority. His massive, six-foot-two muscular body blended in with the surrounding trees. Shadows covered his face, and for a moment, he looked almost terrifying.

Zander's steely eyes locked on hers as he clicked off his phone and shoved it into his pocket. Insecurity shot through her. She didn't have a stitch of makeup on, and had worn her least attractive jogging gear. *Damn the laundry!*

As Zander drew closer, the look in his eyes had her taking a step back. Usually cool-headed and focused, he seemed distracted, off his game... and pissed as hell. Actually, fuming mad was more like it.

He walked up to her. "I'd say good evening, but it doesn't fit."

"No, it doesn't." Raven stepped off the rock and looked up at him, realizing just how tall he was. She stopped cold when she noticed an oozing cut above his eye and a knot just beginning to bruise the side of his face.

"What... you're bleeding... are you okay?"

"Fine."

The sharp, curt tone of his response told her that he didn't want to talk about whatever the hell had just happened to him.

They fell into step together, walking toward the cave entrance. She had to practically jog to keep up with his long stride.

"Team's on their way out. How long ago did you find her?"

"Not fifteen minutes ago." She frowned. "She looks fresh, I'd say within the last twenty-four hours."

His gaze flickered to her tank-top, and she felt a tingle of sexual awareness run over her skin.

"You were out jogging?" He asked.

"Yeah, my ninety-minute hot yoga session this morning just wasn't enough."

Why the hell did she say that?

"A little late in the afternoon for a jog... going to be dark soon."

"I know..."

"You shouldn't be out in the woods after dark. I would've thought you knew that, being a PI and all. Jog a little earlier next time."

She raised her eyebrows. Something was definitely up with him.

He continued, "What brought you to the cave? Off the trail?"

"The buzzards."

"Always the investigator."

She snorted. And yet another zing of embarrassment—a snort? *Really Raven?*

"Did you see anything suspicious this evening? Cars, trucks, people?"

"No. I passed a male jogger on the trail. Baseball cap, dark sunglasses, I'd put him around thirty years old and six feet."

"Did you recognize him?"

"No, but there was a dark blue truck and red sedan at the trailhead when I parked. Guessing the truck belongs to the male jogger, and the sedan is possibly the woman's. Last letters of the truck plate were XPG, and the car, HRR."

His brow cocked. "Good eye, PI. XPG, HRR." He repeated the letters as if etching them into his brain.

"I can run the plates through the DMV, if you'd like."

"I'll handle it." He slowed, surveying the ground.

"I didn't see any tracks, but that doesn't mean they're not there."

"We'll do a thorough search."

They stepped up to the cave entrance. He stopped, paused, and turned to her. "You okay, Rave?"

Rave. Although it was her nickname at work, hearing it come out of his mouth sounded more like something a brother would call their kid sister. His damn kid sister.

She swallowed the lump in her throat that she hadn't even realized was there, and nodded.

Just then, Deena walked out of the cave, shaking her head. She looked up at Zander, and her eyes widened. "What the hell are you doing here?"

"I'm fine."

"You're *fine*?"

"Yep. Hunter's fine, too. The helo's wrecked, though."

"Holy *shit*. Why aren't you home sitting in an ice bath, drinking whiskey from the bottle?" She put her hands on her square hips. "Seriously Zander, I can't believe you're here."

Raven's eyebrows knitted together. "What's going on?"

"Stone here literally just got in a helicopter crash."

"*What?* I thought I heard a helicopter. What were you doing—

"I don't want to talk about it."

Deena stepped forward. "Zander, go home, I've got this."

Zander shook his head, his jaw clenching with anger, or annoyance. Probably both. "I'm not going to tell you again. I'm fine. Just pissed. And I was only a mile away when I got the call about the body, so here I am. It's no big deal."

Deena held up her hands to surrender. "Alright, sorry, no more comments about it."

Zander looked back at her. "I'm going to go take a look."

Deena and Zander descended into the cave, Raven tried to relax the shock from her face.

A helicopter crash? Zander had just fallen from the sky—*literally*—and yet, there he was, responding to the call she'd placed about a dead body. She'd heard he was committed to his job, but this was unbelievable.

Despite the mild temperature, a shiver ran across Raven's skin and she wrapped her arms around herself. Muffled voices echoed from the cave, and flashes of light bounced off the walls where Deena had already begun taking pictures of the scene.

What a night.

Just then, more voices coming from the woods behind her.

"Hey, Raven, a little late to be finding dead bodies in the woods, ain't it?"

Cora McBride, the county medical examiner, stepped over the rocks. Her long, curly, brown hair was tied haphazardly in a knot on the top of her head. She carried a large bag and wore wide-rimmed glasses over tired, shaded eyes. Apparently, she'd been enjoying an evening of relaxation, as well.

"Hey, Cora."

Cora paused, looking Raven up and down. "Why am I

not surprised that you're spending your Sunday evening jogging?"

"Was working a case, unrelated, and besides, it's always good to end the day with some sort of physical activity, Cora."

Cora grinned, and shook her head. "No. No, it's not, Rave. It's always good to end your day with a stiff drink. Which I was in the middle of." She took a deep breath, closed her eyes, and popped her neck from side-to-side. "Okay, game-time, need to focus. In the cave?"

"Yes." Raven followed Cora into the cave, passing Deena on her way out. She blew out a breath as she passed.

The cave was illuminated with flashlights, and standing next to the body, with his fists clenched by his side, Zander's ice-cold gaze shifted to Cora. "Not pretty."

Cora sucked in a breath, then wrinkled her nose at the smell. She yanked on a pair of blue latex gloves as she walked up to the body. "Holy shit."

"Look at the hands."

Raven watched the color fade from Cora's cheeks as she looked down.

"Oh, my *God*. Her fingers have been cut off." She squatted down. Her eyes rounded as she looked at the victim's face. "That's Abby Collier, isn't it? Works at the gym, right?"

"Yes."

Raven frowned. "Who?"

Zander took a step back from the body. "Abby Collier, born and raised here." He paused. "Twenty-one years old."

Twenty-one.

"Looks like she was out jogging, based on the clothes." He nodded.

Cora clicked on her flashlight. "Strangled to death.

Manual strangulation. You can practically see the grip around her neck, from the bruising."

"Can you tell how long she's been deceased?"

"It happened sometime last night. She's in full rigor mortis."

Cora lightly turned the victim's head, where blood matted the curly blonde hair. "She thrashed while whoever did it. Mashed her head into the rock. She fought him."

The words were like ice. Raven's stomach curdled as she imagined the woman—*Abby*—fighting for her life, gasping for air while someone pinned her down and squeezed the life from her. Did she know she was dying? Did she just eventually give up? What are the thoughts that run through a person's head in their last seconds of life?

Cora sat back on her heels and looked at Zander. Her eyes darkened. "Looks like we've got another murder in Devil's Den."

5

$\mathscr{A}$ WET, HEAVY mist hung in the air as Raven turned onto the long driveway that led to Black Rose Investigations.

Darkness had officially fallen.

She flicked on her wipers as she drove under the massive trees that formed a tunnel over the rock driveway. At the end, stood a massive, vine-covered stone mansion, complete with large stone pillars, and an expansive balcony topped with gargoyles that overlooked the grounds. This was her office. Unconventional? Yes, but it was perfect for the kind of work they did—death and darkness were the norm at Black Rose Investigations.

A dim light shone from a second-floor window, but other than that, the house was dark. Which wasn't surprising considering it was almost nine o'clock on Sunday evening.

Most normal people were home, tucking their kids into bed, or settled in their living rooms with a book or glass of wine. Most people hadn't just looked down at the body of a woman who had been strangled to death.

Raven drove around to the back of the house, surprised to see her boss's beat-up truck still sitting outside. That was one of the many things she admired about Dixie—the Knight sisters, Dixie, Roxy, and Scar, had inherited millions of dollars, along with the company, from their parents after they'd died in a tragic plane crash, yet Dixie still chose to drive an old pickup that she'd bought from one of her struggling clients, on the first case Raven had ever worked with her on.

Dixie had recruited Raven just days after graduating college with honors, with a degree in Criminal Justice. Raven jumped at the opportunity and didn't hesitate to leave Texas and move to the small, Southern town of Devil's Den. That was, until she realized just how small it really was. Nestled deep in the Great Shadow Mountains, Devil's Den was full of cowboys, small-town stereotypes, and most notably, decades of folktales about spirits, ghosts, and witches.

Dixie, Roxy, and Scar, and their assistants, Fiona and Harley, were strong, independent, super-smart, badass women, and they'd made Raven feel right at home since her first day on the job. And although it was a far cry from where she grew up, over the last few years, she'd settled in, and had everything in place... except for a man.

She rolled to a stop next to a sports car that she didn't recognize, turned off the engine, grabbed her bag, and yanked up her hood before pushing out of the car. Just as she shut the door, the back door of the house opened, and a disheveled, curvy redhead scooted out the door. The woman was barefoot, with her purse slung over her shoulder, and six-inch red high-heels in her hands.

Raven grinned. "Evening."

The redhead looked up, startled. "Oh. Um, hi. Um..."

Her cheeks turned the color of her heels as she darted into her shiny little sports car.

"Hey, there." Ace Zedler, Black Rose's office manager, super genius, and diehard ladies' man, stood at the back door in nothing but a robe, boxer shorts, slippers, and a beer in his hand. And a grin that stretched from ear to ear.

Raven shook her head as she walked briskly across the driveway. "She's lovely, Ace."

"She sure is."

"Will we ever see her again?"

He sipped his beer. "Who knows."

Raven stepped onto the back porch and stopped in her tracks. A chill snaked up her spine as she stared down at a lifeless, black cat just inches from the doorway.

"What *the hell* is *that*?"

Ace looked down. "Oh, *shit*."

She looked up, her eyes rounded at his casual reaction. "Another one."

"Another one?"

He nodded and grabbed a shovel from behind a potted evergreen. "Yeah, this is the... third one."

"The third what? The third *dead cat*? What the hell are you talking about? Since when?"

"Since our little Eagle Eye Dixie exposed Marden Balik for who she really is."

Raven's mouth dropped open. "Krestel. You're freaking kidding me."

He shook his head, casually scooped up the carcass, and placed it into a black bag. "I wish I were kidding. Krestel's cursed us. All of us. She's cursed Black Rose. Come in. Rain's about to hit." He put the bag in the trash, grabbed her hand and pulled her inside.

"Seriously, there's been three dead cats at our back door since Marden Balik escaped her jail cell?"

"Yep."

"Does everyone know? The whole team?"

"Roxy initially wanted to keep it a secret, so you guys wouldn't get spooked. But then it happened again. So yeah, everyone knows. I think you're the last to find out, actually."

She frowned. "Could just be a coincidence... doesn't actually mean we're cursed."

Ace rolled his eyes. "Whatever you need to tell yourself, Rave. Anyway, nothing we can do about it—just keep an eye out. Keep your head on a swivel."

She shook her head. "This is unbelievable... and fits right into my damn night."

He lifted his drink. "Sounds like you could use a beer."

She raised her eyebrows—*yes*, an ice-cold beer to take the edge off.

As if reading her thoughts, Ace padded across the massive kitchen and pulled a lager from the fridge. He popped the top and handed it to her.

"Thanks."

Ace leaned against the counter, and cocked his head. "Wanna talk about it? What's going on?"

Raven sipped the frothy beer, and closed her eyes for a moment, savoring the split-second of bliss in an evening filled with darkness.

She opened her eyes. "Found a dead girl on the trail, in Hatchet Hollow."

Ace's eyes bugged. *"What?"*

Just then, Dixie walked in with a bag of trash and an armful of dirty coffee mugs. Her long, straight, dark hair was pulled back in a ponytail, accentuating her porcelain skin and almond-shaped eyes, and radiating the beauty that the sisters were known for. Apparently, Dixie had decided to do some much-needed house cleaning on the gloomy Sunday evening.

Dixie's eyes lit up as she saw Raven. "Well good evening, I didn't expect to see..." Her smile faded. "Wait... something's up."

"Raven just found a dead chick in the woods."

Dixie dropped the bag of trash and slid the cups onto the counter. *"What?"*

Raven took another deep sip, praying the buzz would kick in, and begin to numb the adrenaline coursing through her body. "In Hatchet Hollow, just off the trail."

"You're *kidding*. Did you call—

"Of course. Zander, Deena, and Cora are there."

Ace sipped his beer. "Do we know her name?"

"Abby Collier."

"No shit? Yeah..." Ace gazed up at the ceiling, searching his memory. "Yeah, I think I know her. Kinda cute. Well, she used to be, I should say."

"What do you mean, used to be?"

"I've only seen her, occasionally, over the last few months or so, but every time she was wearing all black. Head to toe. And dark makeup. Looked totally different. Gothic."

"Really? This is a change?"

"Oh, yeah, definitely. The dark is definitely new. She used to just look like a normal twenty-something. Always pretty quiet and shy, though."

Dixie leaned against the counter. "So a change in personality, a behavior shift recently..."

"I'd say so."

"Interesting." Dixie turned to Raven. "Tell me everything. What's your initial read?"

The image of Abby Collier's mutilated body flashed through her head. She took a deep breath and then said, "She was wearing exercise clothing. All black come to think of it. Makes me think she was out on the trail, jogging, and taken from there. She was strangled to death—fought through it according to Cora."

"How horrible."

"And... her fingers had been cut off."

"*What?*" Dixie's mouth fell open.

The room fell silent for a moment.

Raven continued, "She had blood coming from her mouth and bruising under her chin, which makes me think she was punched, maybe initially. Maybe knocked out, and then dragged to the cave."

"Was anything else... cut off?"

"No. Not that I could see, anyway."

"Jesus. Did they find the fingers?"

"No."

"Gross. The killer took them with him."

"Possibly. Assuming it's a him."

"Yes, assuming."

"I just can't wrap my head around it..." She paused. "Why the hell would the killer cut them off? I mean, she was tortured enough. Why the fingers?"

Dixie shook her head. "Sick son of a bitch. Crazy, psychotic son of a bitch." She looked at Ace. "Do you know anything else about her? Crazy boyfriend, drugs, anything?"

"Not really. She seemed single—always alone—every time I saw her. And no, my initial impression is that she wasn't into drugs."

"Possibly a random murder."

Raven shifted her weight. "But the fingers... possibly a ritualistic murder."

They sat silent for a minute, as they pondered the question that would no doubt keep them up all night—until Ace's phone dinged. He clicked on the screen, grabbed his beer and began walking out of the kitchen. "Roxy needs me to hack into some FBI case files. See y'all."

After he left, Dixie turned to Raven, and put her hand on her shoulder. "You okay?"

Raven took a deep breath. "It was pretty bad, Dix, I'm not going to lie. But more than that, I just have a feeling... my gut tells me this is no ordinary murder."

Dixie nodded, all too familiar with that feeling. As a private investigator, one of the most important tools is your gut instinct. And the women of Black Rose Investigations were notorious for letting their instincts—their gut—guide them. Sometimes it got them into trouble, but more often than not, it solved complex cases, and put stone-cold killers behind bars.

A faint rumble of thunder sounded in the distance.

Raven set down her beer and gazed outside. "Better get home before the storm hits."

6

$\mathcal{L}$IGHTNING SLICED THE sky as Raven pulled up the rock driveway to her bungalow, nestled at the foot of the tallest mountain in Devil's Den, Black Bear Mountain. The rain was coming down in buckets now, which made the drive home through the curvy roads interesting, to say the least.

She rolled to a stop in front of the house and cursed the rain, kicking herself for not buying a house with a garage. But when she'd moved to Devil's Den the bungalow was the first, and only, house she looked at. From the second she laid eyes on it, she knew she had to have it—it was quaint, warm, welcoming, and within her budget. And thanks to the generous compensation from Black Rose, she purchased it on the spot.

It was a small, two-bedroom, two-bathroom cabin with a wraparound porch. Bright green boxwood shrubs lined the steps that led to the porch, and more color-coordinated pots sat on either side of the front door. When the weather would warm up, she'd plant colorful flowers, and switch out the pots to match, of course. Two vibrant red rocking chairs sat in front of the bay window and matched the red shutters to a tee, which also matched the red threading on the hammock that hung on the edge of the porch. More winter-friendly plants hung from the awnings, spaced exactly fourteen inches apart.

Raven grabbed her bag and bolted across the driveway, jumping over the puddles, then jogged up the porch steps.

Dripping wet, she pushed through the front door and was welcomed by the sweet scent of vanilla, courtesy of the candles she'd purchased the day before. She flicked the lights, grabbed a towel from a decorative basket—that she kept by the door for wet days—and wiped herself down, including the bottom of her shoes. Then, she hung her jacket and bag on the coat rack.

She paused, closed her eyes, and took a deep breath, thankful to be in the sanctuary of her home and out of the rain, the woods, and that godforsaken cave. The image of the lifeless body of Abby Collier flashed through her head and she quickly opened her eyes as a shiver ran across her wet skin.

A drink. She needed a drink—*immediately*.

Raven padded across the shiny, hardwood floor to the kitchen, yanked open the refrigerator door, grabbed a beer and took a long sip. She rested the cold bottle against her temple, leaned against the counter, and gazed out at the dense woods behind her house.

Rain poured down the window.

What a *freaking* night.

Her stomach churned thinking of the sheer violence of Abby's murder. Abby had been out jogging—just as Raven had been—and somehow ended up in a cave fighting for her life. Raven had seen more than a few murder scenes, but only one other scene that involved mutilation. And if this case were no different, she wouldn't be able to sleep for days.

She took another sip and thought of Zander, and how her stomach dropped the moment she saw him walking through the woods. Not that it was an uncommon response to seeing the six-foot-two, muscular Lieutenant with devilishly handsome good looks. Hell, every woman in town drooled over him, including Raven. She'd never forget the first time she met him—it was her first day on the job, and she and Dixie were surveilling a group of small-town drug dealers. One thing led to another, and a fight broke out, and then, seemingly out of nowhere, Zander sprinted up, and single-handedly dismantled the brawl, knocking one thug out, handcuffing the other, and terrifying the third badly enough to pee his pants. Her heart was gone in an instant.

Of course, Raven had never told anyone of her secret crush, or acted on it, for three reasons. One, Zander Stone was like family to the Knight sisters and the last thing she wanted to do was get involved with someone in the "family" at her new job. Two, the women of Black Rose worked very closely with the local law enforcement and she sure as hell didn't need the awkwardness of a break-up if things went south. And three, Zander was at least ten years older than she was, and she got the vibe that he looked at her like a little sister. Little ol' Rave.

She blew out a breath.

In the two short years that she'd lived in Devil's Den, she'd been on a grand total of three dates—*three*. And each had been a blind date, set up by one of the sisters.

The first one, James, was a dentist who was attractive enough, smart enough, ambitious enough, but there had been zero chemistry between them—none. She'd started looking at the clock only fifteen minutes into their first date.

The second date was with a construction worker, who was definitely cute, with an amazing body, but unfortunately, his charm went as far as his IQ—not very.

And the third, the finale of all her dates, the date that had her calling off men, was with a local guitarist—a struggling musician who, she found out at the end of the date, still lived with his mommy. And had a curfew.

But perhaps the most mind-boggling thing about each of the dates was that she found herself thinking of Zander at the end of the night.

How was that even possible? How was it possible to think about, and daydream about, and *fantasize about* someone that she barely knew?

She sighed, and felt a rush of emotions fly through her —the restlessness, unease, and overall creepy feeling that came with seeing a dead body, the sense of urgency to help find whoever the hell did it, and the unexplainable attraction and lust over the Devil's Den Lieutenant, who seemed to dominate her thoughts above all else.

What the hell was it about that guy?

Frustrated, she downed her beer and grabbed another.

It was going to be a long night.

7

*D*AMN THE RAIN, Zander thought as he leapt over a puddle and jogged to his truck. He jumped in and winced at the soreness beginning to settle in his back.

Damn helo crash.

Damn Marden Balik.

Damn Krestel, or whoever the hell she was.

Thank God Hunter knew how to handle the helicopter while it went down in the pitch-black smoke, or whatever the hell it was. Only a few cuts and bruises for the both of them—it could have been a lot worse. And although Zander tried to remind himself of that, and tried to be grateful, he knew that it was just the beginning. The beginning of figuring out what the hell had happened up there. And figuring out where the hell Marden Balik was.

He was soaked to the bone, in pain, hungry, pissed off, and had just added another homicide to his caseload.

Zander turned the ignition and pulled out of the gravel parking lot at the head of Red Rock Trail.

As always, he was the last one to leave the crime scene,

which had taken longer than expected thanks to the relentless downpour.

After Zander and Deena had hustled to take pictures, and search for evidence before the rain picked up, Cora bagged up Abby Collier's body, and promised to begin the autopsy at first light, and he had no doubt that she would.

He gripped the steering wheel.

Another homicide.

Zander approached all crime scenes the same—cool, calm, collected, and with laser focus. But when it came to a homicide, especially involving victims being overpowered by their cowardly attackers, all bets were off. Outside of a crime scene, Zander was known for having a quick temper. A wicked, quick temper. A temper that had almost cost him his job once when he beat a serial rapist within an inch of his life after sexually assaulting a local girl.

Although that fire still burned inside of him, Zander had eventually learned to control his rage, and realized that his time was better spent locking up the son of a bitch, rather than beating him to a pulp. It was his job to serve and protect the citizens of Devil's Den—a town shaded by shadows, that seemed to have more than its fair share of homicides. Zander didn't believe in ghosts and folklore, but he believed in evil, no doubt about that. He'd seen a lot of it in his fifteen years of service, and most cases, he'd never forget.

Due to the small size of the town, and budget constraints, DDPD didn't have a crime scene investigation unit, special task force, or official detectives. The officers of the Devil's Den police department did everything from patrolling, crime scene investigation, evidence collection, and the detective work. They did it all, and they did it well. As police lieutenant, Zander acted as the main detective on all homicides. Sure, he could call in the Sheriff to assist on big cases, but Zander took each case personally, and felt that it was *his* responsibility keep the citizens of Devil's Den safe. He didn't need the Sheriff, or anyone else, barging in and taking over his crime scene.

He turned his windshield wipers on high and hesitated at the four-way stop. He glanced down at the pocket knife in his hand. Usually, he'd wait until morning—a much more respectable time for an unannounced drop-in. But thanks to that damn low-cut tank-top and skin-tight jogging pants she'd been wearing, he couldn't seem to get Raven Cane, or her body, off of his mind.

Maybe the crash did more than rattle his bones.

He was surprised at his reaction to seeing her, standing on top of a rock, in the middle of the woods. Usually, nothing broke his focus at a crime scene, but she had, if even for a split-second. She looked anxious, in shock, but cool-headed, and he swore he saw a spark of... something in her eye when she looked at him. She'd looked so small against the vast landscape, yet somehow strong and deter-mined—and sexy. And he'd been a total dick to her—dammit.

He remembered when she'd moved to town, and he remembered the tingle of excitement that flew through him when he first saw her. And he remembered the metaphor-ical stop sign that appeared above her head when he'd real-ized that she worked for Black Rose Investigations. The ladies of Black Rose were off-limits to him—the Knight sisters were practically family, and they'd have his hide if he went after one of their own. And everyone in town knew that it was never a good idea to piss off one of the Knight sisters.

So as quickly as his attraction had sparked for Raven Cane, he forced it out of his head, only to think of her a few lonely nights when he'd had one too many whiskey drinks. And besides that, he was at least ten years older than she was and he assumed she looked at him like an old man. Ol' Lieutenant Stone.

Zander glanced at the clock—10:30pm.

After another second of hesitation, he flicked on his turn signal and hung a right. The rain blurred his windshield as he drove, a little too fast, through the mountains. He knew the roads by heart—hell, he could drive them with his eyes closed if he really had to.

A bolt of lightning lit the sky as he neared the base of Black Bear Mountain. He braked at the wooden mailbox painted with a vibrant, floral design—he didn't need to check the number, he knew exactly where she lived.

He drove down the long driveway until her small bungalow came into view. A dim light was on. She was up.

Zander parked behind her car, yanked up his collar and got out. The rain pelted his face as he jogged across the driveway and onto the porch. He paused, hesitated again. What the hell was he doing? He should wait until morning...

The door opened.

Dear God, she was still in the tank-top.

He could tell she was surprised to see him, but along with the surprise was the same spark he'd seen in the woods, earlier. Goosebumps prickled his skin, followed by a fleeting moment of embarrassment—why the hell was he reacting so strongly to her all of a sudden?

It had to be that damn tank-top.

He cleared his throat. "Sorry to stop by so late..."

"It's not late. I was up." She looked at his clothes. "You're soaking wet. Come in, out of the rain."

As Zander stepped inside, she grabbed a towel and

handed it to him. He caught the scent of her perfume, or shampoo, or whatever. She smelled like fresh flowers, with a hint of vanilla. And vanilla drove him crazy.

He closed the door behind him, careful to stay on the doormat, and began wiping down his clothes. "I heard you were given your first case. Congratulations."

"Thank you. Stockbrokers are an interesting bunch."

"The Coleman brothers are dicks, and so is Eric. Not hard to imagine insider trading between the three of them."

"I see you've been speaking with Dixie." She stepped back, staring at him standing in her hallway.

He couldn't read her expression, and for some reason, he began to feel slightly awkward. And awkward was not a feeling he was used to.

Maybe he shouldn't have stopped by.

Her gaze shifted to the cut above his eye, and her face filled with concern. "Are you sure you're okay, Zander?"

The damn crash. "Yeah, I'm fine. Just a scratch."

"Okay..."

She stared at him with those big, doe eyes, and suddenly, he forgot why he'd stopped by.

"Would you like a drink?"

Yes. "Sure, thanks."

Raven turned, and his eyes immediately dropped down to her backside—and he felt a tingle in his pants. It was a damn nice ass. A perfectly round, not-too-big, not-too-small, perky little ass.

Get ahold of yourself, Stone.

Zander followed her down the hall, peeling his eyes off of her and glancing around her quaint, little house. Hardwood floors lined the rooms, and large log beams ran across the ceiling. It was cozy—small as shit—but cozy. And clean —as in, not a speck of dirt on the floor, clean. To the right of the entryway was a den with a massive stone fireplace. White candles lined the mantel, and brown leather couches sat on a beige colored rug, with a stack of books on the coffee table—except it wasn't really a stack, the books were staggered on top of each other, each at perfect ninety-degree angles with the bindings facing out.

To the left of the entryway was her office—a spotless desk with a computer and decorative lamp. The wall was lined with shelves, full of storage baskets, each with their own label. He cocked an eyebrow—everything in the house seemed to be strategically placed and organized.

He shook his head. She'd have a heart attack if she saw his place.

She led him into the small kitchen, with dark granite countertops, and dark wood cabinetry. A small seating area sat in front of large windows that looked out to the woods. He liked the kitchen.

He liked looking at her in the kitchen.

"I've got beer, wine, whiskey, and vodka." She pulled open the fridge and looked at him. He had to fight from looking at her chest—he knew what cold air did to a woman's nipples. He glanced at her half-drunk beer on the countertop.

"I'll take a beer, please."

She grabbed a beer, popped the top, and handed it to him. "Did you just leave the cave?"

"Yes." He took a deep sip, and realized just how badly he needed a drink. He was wired, and based on this visit, not making the best decisions. He sipped again.

"Did you find anything else?"

"No, but we'll go back at first light. We verified that the red sedan is her car. We've towed it off and will scan it first thing in the morning."

Raven pushed off the counter and began pacing the room, her wheels turning. "I've been thinking a lot about the fingers. Just seems to throw everything off, right? I mean, why do it?" Pause. "I've thought of two possible scenarios."

"Shoot."

She paced to the end of the kitchen, and the turned back. "It could have some sort of significance to the killer. *Ritual* significance."

"You're talking about Krestel, or witches in general."

"Yes and no. I wouldn't immediately pin Krestel. Mutilation just seems so brutal for a woman. But maybe a male witch?"

"I believe they call that a warlock."

She cocked an eyebrow. "You've been studying up on your witchcraft."

"After decades of living in Devil's Den, you learn these things. Trust me."

"Anyway, there's that. Now to my next possible scenario. Cora believes Abby fought her attacker after she woke up… so she would have fought with her hands, right?"

"Most likely, yeah."

"So then, she would have slapped, punched, scratched at him, right?"

He nodded, and had a feeling he knew where this was going.

"Assuming she scratched his bare skin somewhere on his body, Abby possibly would have gotten the killer's DNA under her fingernails."

"And maybe the killer destroyed the evidence by cutting off her fingers. Is that where you're going with this?"

She stopped in her tracks and turned to him. *"Exactly."*

"Yeah, I've considered the same scenario."

"A smart killer… the worst kind."

He wholeheartedly agreed. The majority of his cases were made up of dumb, idiotic criminals who left a trail of evidence as long as his... you know. But the cases that kept him up at night, the most heinous cases, were always committed by someone smart, clever, self-aware. Cunning.

"In that case, it makes me think that it's got to be someone who knows what they're doing."

"Or just a psycho who watches too many true-crime shows."

"That, too." Pause. "I don't know... it just doesn't sit well with me." After a moment, she said, "Did you find anything else at the scene? Outside the cave?"

He released an exhale and leaned against the counter-top, relieved to be talking through the case, instead of having a bunch of half-developed thoughts jumbled in his head. "We found a few tracks—boot prints—leading away from the cave. We pulled a cast as best we could, but of course, the rain did a number on it." He shook his head, frustrated. "At best, we got half a print."

She paused. "And there's no guarantee that the print even belongs to the killer."

"Right."

"What about the murder weapon? No knife or anything?"

"He murdered her with his hands. But no, we didn't find the knife that was used to cut off her fingers." His tone was almost sarcastic. "Not that damn lucky."

She grabbed her beer. "She wasn't reported missing, was she?"

"No. She wasn't close to her folks, apparently. They didn't talk a lot, especially in the last few months."

"Ace said she'd changed. Started wearing black and became withdrawn."

"That's what her parents said, too."

"Did you speak with them?"

"No, the chief knows the family personally. He made the call tonight."

"How horrible."

It was horrible. The "call" was, without question, the hardest part of his job. And he'd had to make that call more times than he could count. He took a deep breath. "Anyway, we've bagged up her clothes and will send them off first thing in the morning, but aside from the droplets of blood on the shirt—from her chin—there didn't appear to be any bodily fluids on them."

"Maybe they'll find fibers on her shirt, or his hair, maybe."

He nodded, although his gut told him they weren't going to get that lucky with that, either. He continued, "As you probably know, a cave is one of the worst scenarios for trace evidence..."

"The moisture."

"Yep. Even if the killer left a perfect handprint with flashing lights around it, it would be disintegrated by now."

Raven sipped her beer. It was interesting, watching her. She wasn't a blubbering, fearful, shaking mess like most witnesses were after seeing a dead body. No, she was composed, with a determination shining from her eyes— determination to help find whoever killed Abby Collier. But that was *his* job, and he didn't want her anywhere close to a homicide that involved strangling and mutilation.

So he needed to change the subject.

"Anyway..." He reached into his pocket, and pulled out the reason for his visit, which he'd suddenly remembered. "I stopped by to give you this."

Her eyes widened, and she grabbed the pocket knife

from his hands. "I didn't even realize I dropped it." She looked at him. "Where was it?"

"In the cave."

"Thank you so much."

"You're welcome. We were hoping it belonged to our guy, but then I noticed the initials... and I don't see our killer choosing a hot-pink knife, anyway."

She laughed, some of the stress of the day momentarily leaving her face. "No, it's mine—would've been nice if it were the killer's though. No, my dad gave it to me the day I left town."

"To come here?"

She nodded, and for a split-second, he saw sadness in her eyes.

"You miss home?"

"Sometimes, yes, but I'm so lucky to work for Black Rose... I wouldn't change a thing. It just gets kind of lonely out here without family."

Zander glanced around the kitchen for any sign of a man, a boyfriend. It shocked him that she wasn't casually dating someone, at the very least. She was beautiful, with long, straight brown hair, big blue eyes and full pink lips, and he knew the guys of Devil's Den took notice because every man that he worked with drooled over her when she first moved to town.

She continued, "Anyway, he had it specially made with my initials on it. It was sweet."

"Do you take it with you every time you jog?"

She nodded.

"Good. You know how to use it?"

"A pocket knife? Uh, yeah, I know how to use a pocket knife."

He smirked at her sarcastic tone. "No, I mean in a self-defense scenario."

She shrugged. "I mean, it's a knife. I know how to cut something."

He cocked an eyebrow, grinned, and nodded at her finger. "I can see that."

Raven looked down at the bright red slice, still oozing from when she cut it earlier in the woods, and then looked back at him. "How the hell did you notice that?"

"Blame the job."

"Impressive."

"Impressive that while you were under no duress or physical attack, you managed to cut yourself merely by opening your blade? Boy, it *is* a good thing you take that on your jogs with you... for self-defense, of course."

Something in her eye twinkled as she smirked. "Well aren't you a little smartass this evening?"

His eyebrows tipped up, followed by a buzz of enjoyment—Raven Cane had an attitude on her. And he liked it. With his eyes locked on hers, he drained his beer, set it on the table, and motioned her to come to him.

She cocked a brow.

"Come here."

She stared at him for a moment, then set down her beer and walked across the kitchen.

"Turn around."

She grinned, and in an overly accentuated Southern accent said, "But Lieutenant Stone, I've only just met you..."

He laughed. They were definitely flirting now—full-blown flirting. And he liked this, too.

"Seriously. Turn around."

She did as she was told.

"Okay, say your attacker comes at you from behind." He closed the inches between them, pressed up behind her, and wrapped his arms around her. He felt her, ever so slightly, press back into him. His pulse picked up, and he tried to ignore the electricity that was now shooting between them.

He pinned her arms down and had to keep from inhaling the intoxicating scent of her hair. "Can you get to your pocket knife now? You know, the one that you keep for self-defense."

"No... *smartass*."

"Exactly. Lesson one, it's best to run with the knife out, in your hand, or at least have the blade of your keys in your hands, okay?"

"Okay."

She was being submissive and it was making him crazy. He squeezed her harder. "Now, your hands are pinned, and you have no weapon. What's the first thing you do?"

"Scream."

"Good job. Always scream first, as loud as you can. Next, assuming he didn't run away, and still has you from behind, now what?"

No response.

"Drop all of your weight."

She turned her head, her lips inches from his, and he noticed her cheeks were flushed. Was she possibly enjoying this as much as he was? Was she feeling the chemistry between them?

"What do you mean?"

"I mean exactly what I said, drop your weight, but not all the way to the ground. Don't collapse, stay strong, just drop your weight."

She did, and his grip loosened.

He released. "See? The moment you dropped down, I had to bend over to keep my hold on you, which knocked me off balance and caused me to loosen my grip. Always use your attacker's energy, his weight, against him..."

Before he could finish the sentence, she spun on her heel, jabbed him in the ribs with her elbow, and then raised her knee, stopping less than an inch from his groin.

"*WHOA*... whoa, whoa, there." His heart officially stopped beating. "Jesus, Raven."

"Elbow jabs and groin kick... I know what to do from there."

He blew out a breath—*holy shit* that was close—and swallowed the knot in his throat as his pulse came back. "Okay, good job. But don't ever do that again."

She grinned, a gleam in her eye.

He continued, "A jab to the throat works, too." He lightly grabbed her hand. "Jab with a straight hand, not a fist, into the throat."

She nodded.

"Now, let's say you've got your knife out, as you're supposed to, and you're attacked—what do you do now, big shot?"

"Slash the hell out of the son of a bitch."

"Yeah, but where? Always aim for the areas of biggest impact—main arteries, underside of the forearm, eyeballs. The face in general. Slice and jab."

She repeated. "Slice and jab."

"Right." He took a step back. "Show me." He handed her the knife.

She raised her eyebrows.

"Show me."

She cocked her head. "Okay." She flipped open the blade —carefully this time—took a deep breath, and the second she raised her arm, he knocked the knife from her hand, causing it to tumble to the ground, out of her reach.

"Always keep the knife close to your body."

She narrowed her eyes, swooped down and picked it up. And tried again.

"You're holding it wrong." He stepped forward, put his hands over hers. "Run your thumb along the side, like this. Tighten your last three fingers, leave your index finger loose for ease of mobility. Good job."

With his hands over hers, she stared up at him, her big blue eyes wide, her chest rising and falling heavily. He looked down at her, and his gaze trailed to her mouth.

Thunder rumbled outside.

She licked her lips.

He pulled back. *What the hell was he doing?*

Zander cleared his throat, grabbed his beer, and for a moment, the room stood silent.

With apple-red cheeks, and embarrassment written all over her face, she plucked her beer from the counter and took a long sip. "Thanks for the tips."

Tips. He'd like to have given her a different tip... which is exactly why he needed to get the hell out of her house. *Now.*

"Thanks for the beer." He stared at her a moment longer before pulling his keys from his pocket.

"And thanks for bringing me my pocket knife."

He nodded, and paused. For what? Why was he pausing? For her to tug down his jeans, get on her knees, and beg him to stay?

Dammit, this woman was throwing him off, big time.

"Good night, Raven."

She smiled. "Good night, Lieutenant Stone."

Zander felt her eyes on him as he pushed out the front door, and jumped into his truck.

8

RAVEN WOKE UP to her alarm clock screaming at her. She forced her eyes open, rolled over, and glanced at the clock—6:33. She looked out the window. Thanks to the lingering rain, it was still dark outside.

Great.

What she needed was a bright, sunny day. A bright, sunny day to push the darkness of the day before out of her head, and give her a boost of energy after a sleepless night full of tossing and turning, thinking of Abby Collier's vicious murder.

A bright, sunny day to help her focus on all of the work she needed to do, and *not* on Zander Stone.

But it appeared that a sunny day wasn't in the cards.

She threw back the covers, the cool air sweeping across her warm skin. After stepping into her slippers, she pulled on her grey, terry cloth robe. Raven padded to the kitchen, glancing at the front door where not ten hours earlier, Zander's tall, thick body had filled her door frame.

She'd been surprised—*shocked*—when he showed up at her house. And excited. But that excitement was nothing compared to the butterflies she'd gotten when he'd wrapped his arms around her and gave her a lesson on defending herself.

Raven was always a sucker for strong, alpha males, which Zander definitely was—to the extreme. And to have his handsome face and sexy body tossing her around in her kitchen, giving her commands, and teaching her a thing or two, was about all she could handle. There was something erotic about a confident man taking charge, and metaphorically flexing his big muscles... and Zander sure as hell had plenty of muscles to flex. It was everything she could do not to jump him and rip his clothes off.

He was *so damn sexy*, and last night made him even more so.

Raven turned on a dim light, started the coffee, and leaned against the counter.

He could have just dropped off the knife and left. Hell, he didn't even need to come inside. But he did, and he stayed. And despite the horrific afternoon they'd shared, his short visit had turned into a major flirt-fest. Was it possible that Zander thought of her more than a kid? More than little ol' *Rave*?

Her stomach tickled at the thought, but that excitement was immediately replaced by a frown on her face. Regardless if he liked her or not, she knew that her boss wouldn't approve. Zander was off limits.

Without waiting for the brew to finish, grabbed a mug, and poured a steaming cup of coffee. After adding a splash of low-fat creamer and squeeze of honey, she sipped and gazed out the window.

An eerie blue-grey glow began to lighten the woods that surrounded her house.

And suddenly, the hair on the back of her neck prickled.

Was that...?

She squinted and stepped closer to the window. Was... someone out there?

Watching her?

Raven leaned forward and zeroed in on, what appeared to be, a tall, dark figure blending into the shadows, standing motionless, looking right into her window.

No way.

She was tired, seeing things.

She blinked a few times, opened her eyes, and squinted again—the figure was gone.

"You're losing it, Rave."

She shook her head and took a gulp of coffee. She had a busy day ahead of her, and she needed to focus on her first and only case—Eric Stevens, the Coleman brothers, and whether or not they were involved in insider trading. That was going to be her priority today.

Nothing else.

She took a deep breath.

Okay, forget about Abby and focus. Focus Raven.

Raven topped off her coffee, took one more look into the woods and then padded down the hall to the shower.

Sprinkles of rain slid down his windshield as Zander parked under a massive pine tree. It was almost seven in the morning, and although it was wet and gloomy outside, he couldn't wait. He'd been up all night, unable to sleep, thinking about the horrific details of Abby Collier's murder. He needed to get another look at the crime scene, rain or shine, immediately.

He grabbed his gun, flashlight, and just as he was about to push out of the truck door, his cell phone rang.

"Stone."

"Zander, it's Cora."

He straightened. It was early for Cora to be calling him, which made him think she had news. News that couldn't wait.

"Am I calling too early?"

"No, what's up?"

"I couldn't sleep, so I came in super early and started working on Abby's autopsy. I've barely scratched the surface, so to speak, but I've already discovered something interesting, and I had to call."

His pulse picked up. "Okay…"

"Her fingers. First, they were removed post-mortem. It's important to note that they were not removed to inflict pain or torture of any kind because she was already deceased. Second, each finger was severed at the base by a smooth blade, not serrated, as we initially assumed."

"We assumed that because serrated would be easier to cut through bone."

"Exactly. I thought that was weird, right? So I looked closer, and based on the markings, the blade width appears to be wider than a traditional knife…"

"An ax."

Pause. "Or, a *hatchet*."

His eyebrows raised. "You mean to tell me that the killer cut off Abby's fingers with a hatchet, inside Hatchet Hollow."

"Exactly." He could practically hear Cora shudder through the phone. "Looks like we've got a poetic killer on our hands."

A second passed as Zander processed the information.

"Thanks, Cora. Let me know what else you find, immediately."

"Of course." Pause. "Hey, Zander. This makes my skin crawl… just so you know."

He clenched his jaw. "We'll get him, Cora."

"Soon. Bye."

Click.

Zander rested the phone on his chin in deep thought. The fingers were removed post-mortem, which fits the theory that the killer possibly cut them off to destroy evidence that might link back to him.

Raven was right.

A *hatchet.*

Hatchet Hollow.

His gut twisted—A smart, *cocky* killer.

As he got out of the truck, he tried to ignore the pit in his stomach, telling him that this was going to be no ordinary case.

Two hours later, Raven drove up a bumpy driveway that led to a small, decrepit house in the middle of the woods. She cocked an eyebrow as she parked next to a faded sign that was held up only by a stack of rocks.

Claire's Cut and Curl

According to Ace's research, Claire Banks was the name of the hot blonde who received the afternoon delight by Eric Stevens, the day before.

Born and raised in Devil's Den, Claire was a high school dropout, turned salon owner, and had been cutting and coloring hair for the last fifteen years. But Claire's hair cutting abilities wasn't what she was known for. No, according to Ace's thorough research, Claire was known around town for her willingness to have afternoon delights with anyone who was interested. *Anyone, anytime.*

Although Raven's gut told her that Claire knew nothing about Eric's illegal side-job, and most likely wasn't involved in any way whatsoever, she wanted to be sure. And she decided now was as good a time as any to try out her undercover skills.

Raven slid her recorder pen into her breast pocket, grabbed her bag and got out of the car. The lingering rain had finally given up, but the thick clouds remained, making an exceptionally dreary morning.

As she pushed through the old, wooden front door, she was greeted by the smell of chemicals and stale cigarette smoke. She looked around the small salon, which was empty. There were three stations, each with a chair, long mirror, and cabinet. Pictures of women with full, teased hair and neon makeup decorated the walls. *Hello, 1980's.* A layer of dust and hair coated everything—*gross.*

As she closed the door behind her, Claire stepped out of a back room, her eyes wide with surprise... or fear, Raven couldn't decide which. Her hair was in a messy, braided side-ponytail, her eyes bloodshot and shaded. She wore a plaid blouse—unbuttoned to emphasize her impressive cleavage—jeans, and the same bejeweled boots she'd worn the day before.

She looked like she hadn't slept a wink.

Raven's internal radar immediately turned on.

"You have an appointment?" Her voice was clipped as she stood, rigid as a stone, her face pulled tight. Either she'd had some serious Botox, or this woman was having one hell of a morning.

"No. I was hoping to get a trim this morning. Do you

have an open slot?" Raven glanced at the three vacant chairs.

"Looks like it." Her tone dripped with sarcasm. "Have a seat in the first chair by the window. I'll be right back."

No *pleasure to meet you*, or *please take a seat*. No, this woman was strung as tight as a top. And Raven wanted to know why.

As she eased into the ripped, black leather chair, Claire walked up behind her, tying an apron around her neck.

"Just a quick trim?"

"Yes, please."

Claire grabbed a brush from the counter, and it tumbled to the floor.

"Dammit."

Raven watched her cheeks flush as she bent down and picked it up.

"So what's your name?"

"Annabelle Jones."

"Don't recognize the name, or you." She held up the ends of Raven's hair and cocked her head. "Lookin' like a half-inch'll take the dead off."

"Sounds good."

Claire nodded, popped her gum, and Raven caught the faintest scent of liquor.

"You from here?"

"No, I'm new in town, and in the beginning stages of opening my own brokerage firm, actually."

"Brokerage firm, huh?"

Raven noticed Claire slide a nervous glance out the window. Something was up with this woman, no doubt about it. She nodded. "Yep, taking after my daddy."

"We've already got one of those, ya know."

Snip, snip.

Her heart skipped a beat as Claire took off what was, without question, more than a half-inch from the bottom of her hair. She cleared her throat. "I didn't realize there was already a brokerage in town."

Claire snorted. "I wouldn't worry about them, at all. A bunch of good ol' boys operating like it's the eighties. Wouldn't be surprised if they close their doors soon enough."

"Who runs the company?"

"A man named Harold Schumer. Has a team of three, I believe. Handles a lot of business."

Snip, snip, snip.

Raven's heart started racing—dear *God* that was at least *two* inches. She took a quick inhale and returned to the subject. "Actually, that name does ring a bell. Does an Eric Stevens work there?"

Claire glanced up, meeting Raven's gaze in the mirror, and something flickered in her eyes. "Yes."

Raven smiled a sheepish smile. "Cute guy. I ran into him at the grocery store a few weeks ago. We chatted for a moment."

"He's a flirt, no doubt about it. Makes his way around town, for sure."

Raven grinned. "Really?"

Claire cocked an eyebrow and smirked. "Yep. He and I had a little thing, but I've got my eye on someone else now anyway. I can get you his number. I'm sure he'd be more than willing to show you around town." She winked.

"Oh, don't worry about it, I see him from time to time on the trail, too."

The scissors fell from Claire's hand, clattering on the hardwood floor. Her smile faded, her eyes widened, reflecting an undeniable look of fear. She locked eyes with

Raven in the mirror. A moment slid by before she leaned forward, and whispered, "Be careful on that trail, you hear?"

Raven's stomach tickled... the way it did just before she was about to uncover something. Something big. Did Claire know about Abby? Already?

"Why do you say that?"

"Um, just be careful, okay? That's all." She glanced out the window, again, and then swooped down and picked up the scissors. Raven watched her closely in the mirror as she finished up the "trim", her face as pale as a ghost.

"Well, you're all set."

Raven looked at her significantly shorter hair in the mirror. Hiding the shock would be the greatest test of her undercover work this morning. She took a quick breath and smiled. "Looks good, thanks."

Claire set the scissors on the counter as the front door opened. Her head snapped around. A short, brunette woman with hair knotted on the top of her head walked in.

"Oh, hey, Becca, come on in. I'll be with you in a sec." Claire led Raven to the front desk.

As Raven signed the receipt, she felt Claire's steady gaze on her.

"Thanks again."

And as she grabbed her bag, she took a quick glance at the computer screen in the distance, before turning and walking out of the salon.

The door locked behind her as she walked down the porch steps and hit the unlock button on her car. Her mind was reeling as she started the engine.

9

$\mathcal{R}$AVEN GRABBED HER cell phone from the console as she drove down the dirt road.

"Ace here."

"Ace, it's Raven."

"Howdy do?"

"Good. Thanks for getting me the info on Claire Banks, but I need more..."

"You always do."

"I need you to see if there's any connection to Abby Collier. If they're acquaintances, friends, whatever. Check Facebook, etcetera."

"Does this have to do with the Stevens insider trading case?"

Pause. "No... and one more thing."

"Oh, you always have *one more thing*, Raven."

"I need the address to Abby's house."

"I'm not even going to ask."

"Probably best."

"Give me a minute, let me look it up."

Twenty-five seconds later, Ace rattled off the address.

"Thanks, Ace. Let me know what you find out about Claire, okay?"

"You got it. Hey, Rave? Should you be meddling in Abby's case? Shouldn't you be focusing on Eric Stevens?"

She bit her lip. "Just let me know what you find, okay?"

"Alrighty then."

Click.

Raven pulled on her baseball cap, glanced over her shoulder, then pushed out of the car. She looked up at the thick clouds and then at the small apartment building. Her eyes landed on the top, corner unit.

No police cars in the lot, but if she knew Zander, he was still searching the cave for evidence, which was a good thing because he'd kick her ass for showing up at her apartment.

Her stomach clenched—she shouldn't be there. She knew she shouldn't. But this certainly wouldn't be the first time a member of Black Rose Investigations stepped over the line to help solve a case.

And it wouldn't be the last.

She just wanted to take a look around Abby's place.

Just a quick, innocent look.

After one more glance over her shoulder, Raven walked up the short sidewalk leading to the four-unit building. Only a dim light shone from the bottom corner unit, the other two looked unoccupied as far as she could tell.

She jogged up the staircase and slipped on a pair of latex gloves and booties. Then, she pulled a small silver tool—courtesy of Black Rose—from her bag, and without so much of a grunt, popped open the front door.

The smell of burned incense permeated the small studio apartment.

She flicked the light.

The tiny, one-room apartment was divided into three parts—the living area with a small couch, table and television, a sleeping area with a twin size bed, and a kitchen, with the bathroom and laundry room off to the side. It was sparsely decorated with barren walls, dull colors and worn furniture. No pictures of family, no fruity candles, no empty wine bottles, nothing that resembled a normal twenty-one-year-old's home.

Raven examined the doorknob and frame, and then looked around the room—no obvious sign of a break-in, or a struggle of any kind.

She walked to the couch and her eyes immediately landed on a cold cup of tea, and an open book on the coffee table. She picked it up.

The Wiccan Way

Her eyebrows tipped up. Abby had been studying witchcraft the night she was murdered.

As she flipped it open, a small piece of paper tumbled to the floor. She bent over and picked it up.

In shaky cursive were the words—*Great Shadow Book of Secrets.*

"Oh, my..."

Her stomach sank—was it possible that the rumors of the book were true? Does it really exist?

And below that was the letter *K*, circled several times.

Krestel.

After two solid hours of searching the cave—and finding jack-shit—Zander had responded to a four-car pile-up on the slick mountain roads. After that, he hightailed it to Abby

Collier's place to look around, only to be called out to a hold-up at the local bank an hour later.

Now, it was after three o'clock in the afternoon, and it had already been one hell of a day. He was wired, edgy, and pissed as hell that he hadn't been able to fully focus on the Collier case, which had dominated his thoughts all day.

He slipped into his office, and sat down behind his computer just as a pair of knuckles rapped at the door. Officer Luke West, a former green beret, and on his fifth year at the department, poked his head in. "Nice to see you drop in."

Another helicopter crash joke. "Go fuck yourself, West."

Luke grinned, walked inside, and folded his arms across his massive chest. "How you feeling?"

"Fine."

"Come on man, you fell out of the sky less than twenty-four hours ago. You sure you're okay?"

"*Fine.*"

"Alright, alright. Any updates on what the hell happened out there?"

Zander shook his head, grimacing. They'd cleared the wreckage and combed the area but found no signs of a fire whatsoever, or people in black cloaks, or witches for that matter. It was as if the smoke had come from nowhere.

"It's Krestel, man."

Zander felt tension begin to squeeze his shoulders. "Witches," he muttered as he shook his head.

West cocked his head. "What's going on?"

Zander tossed the book he'd found at Abby's apartment on his desk.

"*Beginners guide to Wicca*? You converting?"

"I just found this in Abby Collier's apartment. There were a few others, too."

"No shit?"

"No shit. And there's this..." He tossed the small piece of paper on the desk.

West picked it up. *"Great Shadow Book of Secrets."* His eyes rounded. "And the letter *K*." He looked at Zander. "You know what this is, don't you?"

"Well I'm pretty sure you're going to tell me that the *K* stands for Krestel, right?"

"Dude, that's the least of it. This book?" He raised the piece of paper. "Rumor has it this book contains the most evil curses, hexes and black magic known to mankind. Krestel wrote it, and passes the book to new witches who join her coven. It's a Devil's Den legend. Everyone knows about the book. Of course, some say the book doesn't exist at all." His eyes narrowed. "But others say that this book could destroy us all. Especially if it fell into the wrong hands."

"Aren't Krestel's hands bad enough?"

"She's had the book for decades, if she wanted to destroy us, so to speak, she would have already. But all of her curses and spells are in it—little nasty ones and *big* ones—and her practices, too. Potion brewing, teleportation, clairvoyance, mind control, pyrokinesis, and even necromancy—raising the dead, or demons, from the earth."

"What the hell is pyrokinesis?"

"Control and manipulation of fire."

"Fire." Zander leaned forward, picturing the black smoke exploding from the woods, engulfing the helicopter moments before he and Hunter crashed. "Has anyone ever seen this so-called curse-manual?"

"Not that I'm aware of. You think the witchcraft could have something to do with Abby's murder?"

Zander blew out a breath. "I don't know, man. After

searching her apartment, I spoke with her coworkers at the gym. They were completely shocked. Couldn't think of anyone who would do this to her. She hadn't talked about any arguments or disagreements with anyone lately. No boyfriend, not casually dating anyone. They did say she'd become very withdrawn, *and dark*, the last few months."

"If she was studying to become a witch, that's quite a life change."

"Right."

West paused, then said, "You know, Hatchet Hollow is supposed to be haunted."

"So I hear. But I can tell you one thing, there were no witches hanging out in there when we found the body."

"Maybe you just didn't see them."

Zander shook his head. "Am I the only person around here that doesn't believe in witches, or voodoo, or any of that bullshit?"

West shrugged. "Got to be open-minded, man. Anyway, you find anything else interesting in her apartment?"

"Her laptop. Found her cell phone this morning when we searched her car. Already gave both to Hunter to be analyzed." He leaned back, frustrated. "Either she was meeting up with someone who was up to no good, or someone was stalking her, or she was just in the wrong place at the wrong time"

"So it could have been anyone on the trail that day."

Zander nodded. "There's no security cameras around the trailhead, or parking lot. I've asked Hunter to check with local hunters to see if any have game cameras up in the area."

"What a task."

Zander nodded and glanced out the door as two suits passed by. "Where's our little bank robber?"

"Little Jesse James is booked in cell three. His folks called lawyers." He glanced into the hall. "Who just got here, apparently."

Zander powered on his computer, and shook his head. "Idiot kid. Where the hell did he get a fake gun like that anyway?"

"Bought it online. Looks real, doesn't it?"

He nodded. The seventeen-year-old bank robbing punk had pulled a plastic gun on the bank clerk, demanding every penny in the drawer. The only thing was, the punk hadn't planned on a former green beret to be standing in the next line over. Luke tackled the kid, and had him pig-tied in under a minute. The whole thing had been a shit-show and ate up three damn hours of his life.

"How the hell did you know it was a fake?"

Luke cocked an eyebrow. "Don't insult me."

Just then, Deena popped her head in. "Hey, Stone." She nodded at Luke and then turned back to Zander. "About the guy Raven Cane passed on the trail yesterday morning before she found the body. I did a DMV search of all the local trucks ending in XPG, and compared the height and weight to what Raven remembered, and I got a hit."

"Yeah?"

"Johnny Campos, age twenty-seven, lives a few miles from the trail. He has a record."

"What kind of record?"

"A little B&E, theft... and assault."

"Assault?"

"Yep. Got a little slap-happy with a girlfriend a few years ago."

"Interesting."

"Thought so too. He works at a bar on the outskirts of town."

"Let's check him out, and see if he saw anyone, or anything weird that morning, too."

Deena nodded. "I'll take this one, you've got enough on your plate right now. I'll call you after I chat with him later today."

"Sounds good."

10

Spears of sunlight shot out from the heavy cloud cover as Raven reached the peak of Black Bear Mountain. Dusk was on the horizon, and if the weatherman was correct, more rain was on the way, which would do nothing to help her foul mood and exhaustion, after another long-ass day at work.

After leaving Abby's apartment, Raven had met Dixie at the office to work on all of the other pressing cases they had going on. She hadn't heard anything new regarding the Collier case, nor had she heard from Zander. Not that she expected to—although she'd embarrassingly fantasized about it all day. Despite her hope that maybe, *just maybe*, there was something sparking between them, she reminded herself that Zander had come to her house to return her pocket knife, and that was it. There was nothing else to it.

Nothing else.

But Zander hadn't dominated *all* of her thoughts all day. As much as she'd tried to focus, she couldn't get Abby Collier, or the weird meeting with Claire Banks out of her head. Was there some sort of connection there? Was it possible Claire knew something? And based on what she'd seen on Claire's computer screen on the way out... was it possible that Claire was involved?

And then there was Abby's apartment, and the fact that she had been studying witchcraft. Did that somehow tie into her murder?

She had that nagging feeling that she was missing something, something that was right under her nose. And that feeling drove her absolutely crazy.

Raven parked between two pine trees, got out, and walked across the small gravel parking lot. One positive to the day was that the temperature had climbed to the mid-sixties, which apparently was patio weather according to the ladies of Black Rose. She pushed through the doors of the Black Crow Tavern and inhaled the sweet scent of beer and cedar.

"Hey, Raven girl." Chuck, a proud police veteran, owner of the bar, and Zander Stone's grandfather, smiled and wiped his hands on his apron.

"Hey, Chuck. Good to see you. Scar and Harley here?"

He nodded toward the back. "Since four o'clock. Fiona, too. Out on the patio. I pulled a heater out for them. They've got a pitcher. Want a glass?"

"Yes, please."

He reached into the cooler and handed her an ice-cold pint glass.

"Thanks."

Raven walked through the small, dark bar—which was officially her favorite place in Devil's Den. It was a typical small-town, country bar where everyone knew everyone's name. The renovated log cabin sat on top of the tallest mountain in Devil's Den, Black Bear Mountain, and had a hell of a view of the Great Shadow Mountains. With its dark wood floors, massive log beams, and old street signs, the bar fit right in with the nature that surrounded it.

The bar was also a favorite gathering place of the local police department, and Raven felt a twinge of disappointment when she hadn't seen Zander's jacked-up truck in the parking lot.

She pushed through the back door.

"Hey, Rave!" Harley Quinn, Scar's assistant, rose her pint glass in the air.

Raven smiled as she walked across the patio that stretched under massive Oak trees, strung with lights. The few beams of light from the last of the day's sun shone directly on the table, sparkling off the pitcher of beer.

She carefully looped her bag around the back of a chair and sat down. "Starting early today?"

Harley nodded, her brown, curly hair bouncing on her shoulders. "Team meeting."

"I tagged along." Fiona, Roxy's assistant, grinned, her cat-like green eyes twinkling.

"Anywhere with beer."

Fiona tipped up her glass. "You know me too well."

Scar filled Raven's glass to the brim. "How'd it go with the porn star?"

She sipped, then said, *"Claire."*

"Yeah, Claire. The chick you watched get railed in the woods."

"I *didn't* watch it, okay?"

"Suuuuuure."

"I can tell you one thing for sure, that woman has no part in Eric's insider trading. Eric Stevens is a booty call, that's it." She laughed. "She even offered me his number."

Harley grinned. "You call already?"

Raven rolled her eyes. "Please."

"You need to get laid, Rave. Just sayin'."

Fiona nodded. "No kidding, when was your last date?"

Raven opened her mouth to answer but found herself struggling to remember.

The girls laughed, and Raven rolled her eyes, again.

"Anyway, she's a dead end regarding the Stevens case. But..."

"But what?"

She frowned. "Well... it was odd. When I walked in, she was *extremely* nervous and edgy. Kept looking out the window. Super sketched out."

Scar raised her eyebrows.

She continued, "And I casually mentioned the trail and she freaked."

"I'm sure that reaction was about Abby. The whole town knows about it now." Fiona shivered. "I mean, what a horrific way to go. Strangled and... can you imagine? Her fingers were cut off, one by one."

Raven scrunched her face in disgust. "Believe me, it kept me up all night, imagining it."

"I'm sure it's kept every woman in Devil's Den up all night."

Scar leaned forward. "Does Claire know Abby, maybe?"

"I've already asked Ace to look into that. But," she shifted in her seat. "There's something else. It's probably nothing, and I'm probably totally overthinking it. But as I was leaving, I glanced at her computer screen... she was researching hatchets."

"No *shit?*" Harley and Fiona said, in perfect unison.

"No shit."

"Hatchets, as in, a tool that could have been used to cut off Abby's fingers?"

"Yep."

Harley tapped her glass, in deep thought. "Super sketched out and researching hatchets... seems pretty damn suspicious to me."

Scar began picking her nails, a habit she had when she was thinking through a case. "You need to call Zander."

Raven nodded. She'd already thought about that, but had decided to hold off until the end of the day. Why? She wasn't entirely sure. A little part of her was worried that their flirt-fest the night before would make things awkward between them. And she didn't want to deal with that disappointment until the day was over.

"Have you guys heard anything new about it? About the case? Gossip? Anything?"

Scar shook her head. "No, I heard that Zander didn't find anything else when he went back this morning. But the gossip is crazy. Everyone has their opinions and theories. Krestel did it, or some deranged ex-boyfriend did it, etcetera. Everyone's spooked."

"I'm sure." She stared down at her beer, mindlessly running her finger around the rim, in deep thought.

Fiona glanced at Raven, watched her for a moment. "You're leaving something out."

Scar and Fiona turned to her, eyebrows raised.

She looked up. Uh, well..."

"*Well?*"

"Well I kind of stopped by Abby's apartment this morning. Just to look around."

"Stopped by, as in, broke in and snooped around?"

She cleared her throat. "Yeah." She glanced at Scar, the most senior member of the Black Rose team at the table, who had reprimanded her for much less.

The corner of Scar's lip curled up. "What happens, *or is*

said, at the Black Crow Tavern, stays at the Black Crow Tavern."

Raven smiled. "Thanks." She exhaled loudly, relieved to be able to talk about what she saw. "You're not going to believe this. Abby had been studying witchcraft before she was murdered."

"*What?* No way."

"Way. And... on a small piece of paper, hidden in a book, she'd scribbled *Great Shadow Book of Secrets*, with the letter *K* underneath."

Scar's mouth dropped open.

Harley set down her drink, her eyes the size of golf balls. "Are you serious?"

"Yeah."

Scar leaned forward, urgency pitching in her voice. "Was it there? Was the book there? Did you see it?"

Raven shook her head. "No, no, just the note. I left it, for Zander to find."

"Oh, my God. That book..." Her eyes darkened. "Is pure evil."

"I know. I've heard. Do you think it really exists?"

No one responded. They looked around at each other, not wanting to admit that it was a very real possibility.

The table sat silent for a moment, and Raven's gut twisted. She drained her drink and pushed away from the table.

"Where're you going?"

She grabbed her bag. "I've got to check on something before the sun goes down."

Twenty minutes later, Raven parked under the same pine trees that she'd parked under not twenty-four hours earlier—thirty minutes before she found Abby Collier's body.

She glanced at the woods, and the creepy feeling of deja vu had her shifting in her seat. It was almost the exact time she'd gotten there yesterday, and the weather was eerily similar too—thick, ominous clouds, which only added to the overall creepiness that had fallen over the town in the last twenty-four hours. She glanced around and noted two cars, a beat-up hatchback, and an extended cab Chevy. She reached back, plucked her bag from the backseat, and took one more glance around and got out.

She hesitated, then shook her head and began walking across the soggy ground. This was her job—solving mysteries is what she did 24/7. Solving mysteries is what made her tick, for better or worse. She couldn't ignore the nagging feeling, screaming at her that they were missing something in that damn cave.

So here she was, taking it upon herself to check it out.

Abby Collier deserved justice. Abby Collier deserved another set of eyes on that cave, and by God, she was going to give it to her.

A warm breeze swept across her skin as she stepped onto the darkening trail. She glanced at her watch—almost seven, about an hour before nightfall. Nervously, she felt for her Glock in the front pocket of her bag to confirm it was still there—yep, it was. It hadn't grown legs and sauntered away.

Dammit, she was edgy.

Raven pulled her pocket knife from her pocket, flipped it open, and gripped it as Zander had taught her. And then said a little prayer that her grip wouldn't matter because she'd, hopefully, never be put in a self-defense scenario.

She smiled at the young mom pushing a double stroller,

packed with two young boys munching on graham crackers. A split-second of envy zipped through her as she imagined herself, going out for an evening jog with her two boys, before going home and making dinner for her handsome husband... her handsome *doctor* husband. No, *surgeon* husband. *Yes*—former Navy SEAL, turned plastic surgeon, husband. Yeah, that's it.

Her life was so different from the young joggers'. Her days were spent investigating dozens of different cases, more often than not including a dead body, and her evenings were spent catching up on laundry or clicking through the television while eating a frozen dinner.

As much as she hated to admit it, she was lonely. Not all the time, but as the years of her life clicked by, there were more nights than not that she wished she'd had a man to fall asleep beside.

To hold her, love her.

Keep her safe.

Her thoughts shifted to Zander. What were his evenings like? Did he have a girlfriend? She knew he'd never married, but she'd be shocked if he didn't have a woman, or a booty call, at least. The women of Devil's Den swooned over Zander, and she couldn't blame them. Yep, he probably spent his evenings having multiple ménage-a-trois' with the most beautiful women in the tristate area—not uptight, perfectionist, private investigators with a penchant for cheap beer and label makers.

Heat rose to her cheeks as she thought of his arms around her the night before. During their flirt-fest, she'd sworn he felt their chemistry, too. She saw it in his eyes— right before he clammed up and bolted out the front door.

She sighed.

Her gaze shifted to another jogger, a woman, in the

distance. For a second, she considered stopping the lone jogger and telling her to get home, be vigilant, and stay off the trail. Exactly as Claire Banks had said to her.

She frowned, shook her head. Claire knew *something*. She was one-hundred percent sure of it. She just didn't know what that something was, or how it tied in.

The woman zipped past her just as Raven veered off the trail into the woods. Her stomach tickled with nerves as she stepped through the thick brush. It was creepy. Dark shadows stretched across the forest floor, dancing in the breeze, like ghosts, watching her.

Baiting her.

She took a deep breath.

Calm down, Raven.

All of a sudden—*snick.*

Raven stopped, looked over her shoulder.

No one.

A gust of wind blew past her, spinning dead leaves across her body.

Was she being followed?

Raven glanced from tree to tree, where the shadows continued to sway eerily from side to side. Goosebumps spread over her arms. She felt... something.

A presence.

Her pulse picked up.

She listened to the whistle of the wind through the trees. No turning back now. Hatchet Hollow was only a few yards away.

Raven gripped the pocket knife in her hand and pushed on, her heart beginning to race in her chest.

She took a wary look over her shoulder and couldn't shake the feeling that she was being followed—that she wasn't the only person in the woods.

Raven pressed into a brisk walk, almost a jog, until the rocks came into view. Yellow police tape roped off the area just in front of the cave.

Do not cross.

She stepped onto the large rock and took another glance over her shoulder.

Get in, get out, Rave.

She stepped off the rock, pulled a flashlight from her bag, and stepped inside.

The hair on the back of her neck stood up.

Abby Collier's body was gone, but death hung like a wet blanket in the air. A heavy, moldy blanket.

Focus.

The faint sound of dripping water drummed in her ears as she carefully walked across the cave, slowly sweeping the light from side to side.

What were they missing? What was she looking for?

Raven shined the light along the sides of the cave, the slick, wet walls reflecting in the beam. She panned to the smooth rock in the corner where Abby's body lay twenty-four hours ago. She frowned, kneeled down.

Three red puddles stained the rock from where the blood had trickled from Abby's mouth and her fingers had been sawed from her hands. She pulled a latex glove from her bag, slipped it on, and traced her finger across the smooth cave floor. She imagined what it must have felt like, being pinned against the cold rock, strangled. She sifted through a pile of flint stone.

Raven sat back on her heels and shined the light around.

Something sparkled in the beam.

She frowned and squinted at the tiny reflection in the corner. What the hell was that? Raven pushed off the floor and walked to the object, just inches from where Abby's body was found. She crouched down.

A tiny sliver of teal fabric with reflective coating was pinned under a rock.

She cocked her head. It looked like fabric from exercise clothes. But Abby's clothes were black—black jogging pants, black T-shirt and black sports bra—no teal. She grabbed an evidence bag, tweezers, and carefully plucked the fabric from the crevasse.

Just as she zipped it up, she felt a breeze of movement behind her. Ice-cold fear shot through her. She surged to her feet and turned around, so sure that she was about to be face-to-face with the killer.

But there was no one.

Her hand trembled as she shined the light around the cave. Her heart felt like it was about to burst out of her chest.

Time to get the hell out of here, now.

Raven grabbed her bag and jogged across the cave, her skin practically crawling with fright. With each step her fear intensified, her instinct telling her that she was in grave danger. She leapt out of the cave, and didn't stop—it was as if two large hands were grabbing for her from behind, so close, just inches away.

Her heart raced as she jumped onto the rock, and then down onto the forest floor. The woods had darkened during her short time in the cave. She took off, with just the dim glow of twilight illuminating her way.

Her gaze snapped toward every dark shadow that seemed to be playing tricks on her.

Holy shit, she was *scared.*

Suddenly, she heard voices—whispers—around her.

Panic bubbled up, and she pushed into a sprint.

Her toe caught a root, and she lurched forward, tumbling to the ground, her bag flying a few feet in front of her. Pain zinged her knee, but she jumped up and glanced behind her.

She paused.

Was that...?

Raven squinted, and swore she saw a dark silhouette slowly fade into Hatchet Hollow.

11

RAVEN WIPED THE sweat from her brow and pushed through the shiny doors of the massive, sprawling building that was home to Graves Laboratory, a top of the line, full-service forensics lab. Her steps were unsteadied, her hands still trembling from the incident she'd just had in the woods. After she'd arrived safely to her car, she sat in the driver's seat for a solid minute, practicing her yoga breathing, trying to calm down. She was drenched in sweat and scared out of her mind, and although all she wanted to do was go home and hide under the covers, she had something more important to do—and it couldn't wait.

The expansive lobby was empty, with only the dim glow of the after-hours lights. She looked around as she walked across the shiny, marble floors. No matter how many times she'd been to Graves, she was always awestruck at the beauty of the building. She glanced out the floor-to-ceiling windows, into the darkness, and her stomach sank with the same feeling she had in the woods. A feeling that someone was watching her. Waiting for her.

Dammit, she wanted to get home. And she would, right after this.

The large clock on the wall ticked to seven as she walked up to the reception desk, which was unmanned, and pressed the after-hours button.

Graves was a lot like Black Rose—full of over-committed workaholics who worked twenty-four hours a day, even though they technically didn't have to. Black Rose used Graves exclusively for their cases and were on a first-name basis with most of the staff.

A minute ticked by.

Finally, a sultry, female voice came through the speaker.

"How may I help you?"

"Hi, it's Raven from Black Rose Investigations. Any chance Max is around?"

"Just a moment, please."

She leaned against the counter, and pulled out her cell phone as she waited—one new message. She clicked it open.

FYI, so far, I can't find any connection between Abby Collier and Claire Banks. Will keep looking and let you know if I find anything. -Ace

No connection. She frowned. Maybe she was just over-thinking things. Maybe Claire was just having a bad day. Maybe she didn't know a damn thing. Maybe Raven's gut was wrong.

Suddenly, the door buzzed.

"Go on up, Miss Cane."

"Thank you."

The elevator zipped her to the top floor, and the doors slid open. The floor was dark and quiet. She walked down the hall to the last office and peeked inside as she quietly knocked.

"Miss Cane, to what do I owe this pleasure?" Max Blackwood, a former forensic medical examiner, now the director of Graves, stood from his chair. He wore an expensive navy-blue suit, and she smiled at the opened beer on his desk.

An eternal bachelor with a penchant for high-dollar coffee, Max was known for two things—being a literal genius, and his bad luck with women, which surprised Raven considering the guy looked like he'd just stepped out of GQ magazine.

"Sorry it's so late."

He smiled and walked around to the front of his desk. "No worries, I'm working late, as always."

She nodded at the bottle. "Beer always helps."

"It sure does. Keeps the juices flowing. Would you like one?"

"No, thanks, this is a quick visit."

"What can I help you with?"

She reached into her bag and held up the evidence bag.

"This piece of fabric... looks like material from exercise clothes to me."

He frowned, took the bag, and held it up for a closer look. "I'm assuming you want me to scan it for DNA?"

"Exactly."

"May I ask where it's from?"

"I found it in Hatchet Hollow, where Abby Collier's body was just found. It's probably nothing at all, but it caught my eye, so here I am."

He shook his head. "So sad. The whole town is spooked." He looked closer. "Looks like it's been there awhile, and I'll bet the moisture from the cave has done a number on any DNA, assuming there's any on it, of course."

He looked at her, and the corner of his lip curled up. "But I sure do love a challenge."

Relief washed over her. "Thanks, Max. Can you look at it soon, like, tonight or tomorrow?"

He cocked an eyebrow. "That'll cost you, Miss Cane."

She grinned. "How many caramel macchiatos?"

"Two." A devilish smile crossed his face. "And my file cabinet is in dire need of organization."

Apparently, her incessant need for organization and structure preceded her.

She glanced at the cabinet, which had folders sticking haphazardly out of the drawers.

She sighed. "Done."

12

ZANDER WALKED OUT of the station doors and stepped onto the parking lot. A gust of wind whipped past him, and he zipped up his coat. It was just past nine o'clock and it had turned into a cool, dark night, just like his mood.

Zander needed three things—a break from his office, food, and a long-ass shower. And then, he'd drive himself right back to the station to work on Abby Collier's case, for hours into the night.

But first, he just needed a damn hour.

His phone rang.

"Stone here."

"Zander, it's Deena. Just left the bar where Johnny Campos works, and let me tell you, that place is as seedy as it gets."

"So you're telling me you drank a few pints while you were there."

"Two. And one shot."

Zander laughed.

"Anyway, I talked to our boy. He confirmed that it was his

truck that Raven saw parked in the lot. Says he didn't see anyone or anything suspicious Sunday morning."

"Damn."

"I also asked him about Saturday specifically. Say's he worked the day shift—yeah, the bar opens at ten in the morning—then went home."

"Sounds like you interviewed the poor kid."

"Well, I just had a weird feeling—he's got a rap sheet and no apparent alibi for Saturday night. My guts telling me to look deeper into this guy."

Zander tugged up his coat collar to block the wind. "We're going to need a hell of a lot more than just the fact that he has a rap sheet, and was jogging on a public trail the day after Abby's murder to consider him a suspect—*at all*."

"Let me look into him a little more before you write him off. My radar's going off like crazy."

"Be my guest. Start with his residence, see if there are any cameras to confirm that he didn't leave Saturday night."

"You got it. See ya."

Click.

Zander jumped into his truck as his phone beeped—he must've missed a call while he was on the phone with Deena. He dialed the number.

"Cora here.

"Hey, it's Stone."

"Good, thanks for calling me back so quickly. First, I got the tox back. Abby was clean."

"No drugs or alcohol in her system?"

"Nope."

"Interesting."

"Also, I confirmed that the bruising on her jaw happened before she was killed."

"Son of a bitch punched her, knocked her out."

"Appears that way. The autopsy isn't fully complete yet, but I wanted to talk through something with you, more or less."

"Talk through something?"

"Yeah. Do you remember the Marsha Welch murder two years ago?"

Zander's stomach clenched. "Yeah, I remember."

"Went cold, right?"

"Right. Never found her cell phone, her laptop was for school mainly and didn't turn up any clues. Parents knew nothing. Her friends knew nothing. We literally had nothing to go on."

"And she was strangled to death and found in the woods. She'd been knocked out with chloroform."

"Right."

"Well, I just found traces of moonmilk on Abby's body—

"Moonmilk?"

"Yeah, moonmilk."

"What the hell is moonmilk?"

"Oh, sorry. Moonmilk is a white, sticky substance made up of fine crystals of carbonates, found primarily in caves. I've confirmed it's in Hatchet Hollow."

"Okay..."

"As I was saying, we found some on Abby's body, and it immediately reminded me of Marsha's autopsy. I'm sure you remember, but moonmilk was also found on her body, although she wasn't found in a cave."

He frowned, paused—he remembered every piece of Marsha Welch's case file but finding a white sticky substance made up of carbonates didn't ring a bell. *At all.* No, he'd never heard the word moonmilk before in his life.

"Are you sure?"

"Sure about what? That moonmilk was found on both their bodies?"

"Yeah."

"I'm one-hundred percent sure. I'm looking at Marsha Welch's autopsy report right now. And both victims were around the same age, young women, strangled to death. The only difference is that Marsha's fingers weren't cut off."

"There'd be no reason to cut them off if she didn't fight him."

"And she didn't fight because she was knocked out from the chloroform."

"Right." Pause. "And we never determined the place of Marsha's murder... only that she definitely wasn't killed where we found her."

"So she was killed somewhere else and then dumped in the woods."

"To throw us off."

"Agreed. Hell, Zander, maybe she was killed in Hatchet Hollow. By the same freaking person."

A moment of silence ticked by.

"Do you know if Marsha was into witchcraft, at all? Or anything like that?"

"No, I don't think so. I mean, it doesn't ring a bell."

"Can you resend Marsha's full autopsy report?"

"No problem, give me a quick second." Zander heard the *click, click, click* of Cora's computer. "And... there. Sent. It should be in your inbox. Also, one more thing. There's no traces of semen anywhere on, or in Abby's body, so she hadn't been with anyone lately."

He assumed that, but was hoping they'd have someone else to interview, at least. "Okay, thanks, Cora."

"No problem. Hopefully Max will pull something useful from that fabric."

"What fabric?"

"The piece that Raven brought to him a bit ago, that she found in the cave. He called me about something unrelated, and we started talking about Abby, and he just mentioned it."

"Raven found a piece of fabric? *In the cave?*"

"That's what he said. Not even two hours ago."

Zander felt his cheeks heat with anger. Why the hell didn't she call him? Why the hell didn't she let him handle it? Why the *fuck* did she go back to the cave?

"Thanks, Cora. Let me know when you have the final report done."

"Will do."

Aggravated, he tossed the phone on the passenger seat and pulled out of the parking lot.

What the hell was Raven doing going back to the scene of a grisly murder? By herself? He surprised himself when a surge of protectiveness overcame him. He didn't want Raven involved in this case. He didn't want her anywhere close to where a woman was mutilated and strangled to death.

He took a deep breath, his mind racing.

Moonmilk.

Moonmilk?

He frowned—he definitely would have remembered that detail from Marsha's case, even if it were almost two years ago. Surely he would have. Right?

The location of Marsha's body was found a half-mile from the cave. Could the piece of fabric Raven found possibly belong to her? Was it possible that the same person who killed Abby Collier, also killed Marsha Welch?

He gripped the steering wheel as confusion, frustration, and anger began to mix with the starvation and exhaustion that had already settled in.

He gritted his teeth.

Dammit!

He slammed the brakes, shoved the truck into reverse, and slid back into the parking lot. With the truck running, he scaled the station steps and jogged into his office.

He flicked on the light, sank into his chair, and turned on the computer that he had just turned off five minutes earlier. He clicked on his email and opened the latest one from Cora. He skimmed through Marsha's autopsy report and stopped cold.

He frowned and leaned forward—there it was, Cora's findings of moonmilk on Marsha's body.

What the hell?

It was as if it were the first time he was reading the information.

He grabbed his keys and pushed out of the chair.

13

———

*R*AVEN PUT THE full weight of her body against the door as she flung her keys and bag on the floor. She closed her eyes and took a deep breath.

Home.

She was *home*—away from the cave, the murder, the chaos.

Her eyes drifted open to her bag and all the contents sprawled out on the floor.

Leave it. Don't be so damn neurotic. Just leave it.

A minute ticked by as she stared at the mess.

Her skin began to crawl.

A few more seconds passed as she argued with herself in her head. *Just leave it. What's the worst that could happen? You're such a nutcase.*

With an eye roll, Raven bent down, picked up her belongings, and hung them neatly on the coat rack.

Well, she lost that battle.

She sighed and walked to the kitchen. A drink was exactly what she needed.

Raven turned on the light, and her heart stopped.

The kitchen window was open, just a crack. And she never, *ever*, forgot to close, and lock, the windows and doors before leaving the house.

Her eyes darted around the room. Nothing appeared to be stolen, out of place, or knocked over, and the back door was locked.

Raven pulled down an extra gun that she kept on top of the refrigerator, cocked it, and then quickly closed—and locked—the window. She grabbed her cell phone and dialed 911, but didn't connect. With the gun in one hand, and her finger hovering above the call button on her phone in the other, she stepped out of the kitchen.

The silence was deafening as she tiptoed down the hall. She peered into her office—her laptop was still there, closed, and powered off. Okay, so this definitely wasn't a burglary.

She turned, glanced into the den—nothing out of sorts —before walking to her bedroom. With all senses piqued, she slowly pushed open the door and turned on the light.

Her stomach hit the floor as her eyes locked on the small, grey stone lying in the center of her bed.

Raven didn't need to look closer. She didn't need to pick it up—she had absolutely no doubt that the stone was from the cave where Abby Collier took her last breath.

Ding, ding.

She jumped, nearly screaming at the sound of the doorbell.

Her heart began to race.

Who the hell would be visiting her now?

She looked back at the stone on her bed. What the hell was happening?

Her finger slid over the trigger as she tiptoed down the hall.

Ding, ding.

She held her breath and looked through the peephole.

Zander.

And the man looked pissed as hell.

Raven slid the gun on the windowsill, and put her phone into her pocket. Taking a deep breath, she opened the door, and tensed at the stone-cold look in his eyes.

"What the *hell* were you doing going back to the cave? *By yourself,*" he seethed.

Obviously, Zander had found out about her trip to Graves earlier. *Fan-freaking-tastic.*

Before she could respond, he frowned, looked her up and down. "Wait, what's wrong?"

"Nothing. You just startled me, is all."

"You're as white as a ghost. What's wrong?" He stepped inside, his tall, muscular body filling the foyer.

Raven swallowed the knot in her throat, blew out a breath, and motioned him to follow her. She felt his eyes burning into her back as she stepped into the bedroom.

He stood beside her and followed her gaze. "What is that? A rock?" He looked at her, then back at the grey stone on her bed.

"Yeah. It was here when I got home, just a few minutes ago."

His eyes narrowed. "You think someone put it there?"

"I want to say no. I want to say there's a chance that it fell off my shoe or something, but no it wasn't there earlier."

He turned to her, with laser focus. "You think someone broke in?"

Pause. "Possibly."

"You mean to tell me that you went to Hatchet Hollow, then to Graves to drop off a piece of evidence you found, and when you came home, it was there."

Her chest squeezed at the realization of what was happening. Yes, someone had been watching her, following her. Someone knew she went to the cave and found something. And someone wanted to make sure that she knew, that they knew.

His eyes flared with anger. "Raven, you've got to stay out of this, do you understand?"

Raven. Not Rave.

"Do you understand?"

She glowered back at him.

"You cannot go back to that cave. You understand? I'm not asking you, I'm telling you." He ran his fingers through his hair. "Do you remember Marsha Welch?"

She searched her memory. "I'd just moved here. Yeah, I remember. She was found in the woods, about two years ago." Her eyes widened. "Close to Hatchet Hollow, right?"

"Right."

"Oh, my God... do you think..."

"I don't know, but it's enough to make me tell you to stay the hell away from there." He looked back at the stone. "And you're sure as hell not staying here tonight."

"Who says?"

"*I say.*" His eyes locked on hers and his brows raised slightly, punctuating the authority in his voice. Zander Stone was not used to people defying his requests—that much was obvious.

She stared at him for a moment, not sure what to say next. This was only the second time he'd been to her house, and it was the second time in just two days. He could have called about the fabric. He could have met her at the office, but instead, there he was, standing in her bedroom, telling her what she can, and cannot do.

He narrowed his eyes. "Look, I've worked with Black

Rose since I started this job. I understand the commitment it takes to be a part of the team, and, Raven, I know how committed you are to your job. But this is too much. This isn't your damn case! Someone broke into your house and left you a warning. A warning to stay away. And Raven?" He squared his shoulders. "You *will* stay the hell away. I won't have you getting hurt." He paused, and shifted his weight. "I also understand the delicacy between a private investigator and law enforcement—I get it. But what I don't get, and what I won't tolerate, is anyone withholding evidence from one of my cases that could help put a murderer behind bars. You should have called me about the fabric—should have let me handle it."

She felt her cheeks heat. He was right on all counts, but she'd be damned if she allowed him to stand in her bedroom, *in her house*, and treat her like a child. Scolding her like a toddler.

Raven's pulse pounded, and before she could say one of the hundred obscenities that were rolling around in her head, his phone rang.

He didn't move a muscle—his eyes remained locked on hers, waiting for her to say something.

Yes sir, probably.

Three rings passed.

"Aren't you going to get that?"

He grabbed the phone from his belt. "What?... What, where..."

She watched his face fade from anger, to surprise, to an icy focus, and her stomach sank. Something had happened. Something bad.

"...I'll be there in five. And Hunter, send West to 928 Black Bear Road, Raven Cane's house. She had a break-in this evening. Scan the house and look for fingerprints. And bag up the stone that was left."

Click.

"What's happened?"

He looked at her, hesitated.

"Zander, what's happened? Another body?"

The twitch in his jaw told her everything she needed to know.

She covered her mouth and whispered, "Oh, my..."

Zander glanced at her bed, then back at her. "West will be here within five minutes. Pack a bag. You're not staying here."

He didn't wait for a response. He turned and left the room, and she called out after him.

"I don't need West to come. I can dust for fingerprints myself. Just let me..."

He whipped around. "Leave it to us, Raven. I'm serious."

And with that, he turned around and jogged out the front door.

Raven's heart raced with adrenaline as she watched his taillights fade into the distance. She took a deep breath.

What a night.

Silence buzzed in her ears as she slowly turned.

Someone had been watching her. Someone broke into her house. Someone wanted to send her a message.

Zander was right. She *was* getting too close.

Dammit!

She stomped down the hall, into the kitchen, and noticed her phone was illuminated on the counter. She picked it up —one missed call, one voicemail, fifty-eight minutes ago.

Raven looked at the caller ID.

Claire Banks.

14

ZANDER FLICKED ON his high beams as he bounced down the pitted dirt road. Dense woods surrounded him, pitch-black in the night.

He glanced at the clock as the adrenaline pulsed through his veins—10:30pm.

Another fucking body.

Rain dotted his windshield as he rolled to a stop behind Hunter's patrol car, which was parked behind an ambulance.

Bright lights shot out from behind the small cabin, outlining the steep roof and crooked chimney—apparently the victim was found outside.

He took a quick deep breath, shoved the truck into park, grabbed his jacket, and got out.

"Stone." Deena emerged from the woods. She shook her head. "Not pretty."

"Where is she?"

They fell into step together, walking up the rock driveway.

"Backyard."

Voices echoed through the wind as they came up on the side of the house.

"How long ago?"

"Her friend, Becca, found her about thirty minutes ago. Said she'd just spoken to her over the phone a few hours ago. She's fresh. Within the last hour."

"What was the friend doing here?"

"They had planned a girls' night, watching reality shows or whatever."

Zander flipped up his collar as he rounded the corner to the back of the house. The rain was already starting to pick up. Multiple klieg lights illuminated a pale body on the ground, just feet from a shiny red sports car.

"Found next to her car?"

Deena nodded. "Friend says she was on her way to make a quick liquor run. We're assuming that's when she got attacked."

"Hey, Stone."

Zander nodded at Hunter, who was taking pictures of the scene.

His stomach sank as he looked down at the young woman, sprawled out on the wet ground. Her blonde hair was matted with dirt and mud. Her bloodshot eyes were open, staring directly at him.

"Claire Banks."

Hunter nodded.

Although he didn't even need to check, his gaze shifted to her hands, where each of her fingers had been severed off.

He shook his head and kneeled down, taking note of the bright red marks around her neck.

Manual strangulation, and severed fingers.

Just like Abby Collier.

Anger boiled in his system. He looked over his shoulder at Deena and Hunter. "Get a tent over here, immediately. This rain is going to pick up."

"On it." Deena took off toward her car as Hunter kneeled down next to Zander.

"Two."

Zander slowly nodded. "Two."

A moment of silence ticked by, neither one wanting to acknowledge that the same person who killed Abby Collier, had just killed again.

It was just past one in the morning by the time Zander got into his truck. They'd spent the last three hours searching Claire Banks's home, yard, and car, looking for anything that might lead them to whoever the hell brutally ended her life.

They'd found nothing.

Her body was tagged, bagged, and sent off for an autopsy slated to begin at first light.

He gripped the steering wheel so tight that his knuckles turned white as he drove down the dirt road.

A serial killer.

A serial killer in Devil's Den.

A serial killer who possibly had their sights set on Raven Cane.

The thought made him want to vomit, right after punching a hole through the wall.

What was it about this girl that had him completely consumed, completely infatuated? Completely unable to concentrate on anything other than keeping her safe?

Over the last three hours, his thoughts had trailed to Raven more times than he cared to admit. He'd even texted West—three separate times—to confirm that he was there, at her house, and that she was okay. West's last text was thirty minutes ago, telling Zander that he was about to hit the road, and not surprisingly, Raven refused to leave her house.

What the hell? Why was she so stubborn?

Zander clicked on his cell phone and scrolled to her number, but paused. He couldn't *make* her leave her house and stay somewhere else. And where would she stay anyway? Zander got the vibe that Raven didn't have many friends—her work was her best friend.

He stopped at a four-way and hesitated.

A minute ticked by, and with a groan, he flicked on his turn signal and turned left toward Black Bear Mountain.

Dammit, Zander.

15

___

CLUTCHING A GLASS of whiskey—because that was the only booze that would do at that moment —Raven took a break from pacing a hole in the living room, to lean up against the window and watch the lightning outside.

Another storm was blowing in.

It was just past one in the morning, and not surprisingly, sleep was the last thing on her mind.

Officer West had left thirty minutes earlier, after sweeping the house for evidence, scanning for fingerprints, and bagging up the grey stone for analysis. They determined that whoever broke in, came in through the unlocked kitchen window—adding embarrassment to an already horrible evening. It wasn't like her to leave the house unlocked, which meant only one thing—she was extremely distracted.

They'd found no prints, or anything useful, at all. And after hours of *babysitting* her, West had finally left her alone —to her own peril, he'd jokingly said as he walked out the door.

Lightning pierced the dark sky outside, followed by the pitter-patter of raindrops.

She clicked on her phone and listened to the voicemail for what seemed like the hundredth time.

"Miss Cane, nice undercover work at my shop yesterday. My friend, Becca, saw you leaving and informed me that you really work for Black Rose Investigations." Pause. *"I can only assume that you came to visit me to discuss what I saw Sunday night."* Her voice started to shake. *"I want to meet... I'm not comfortable discussing this over the phone, considering who it is."*

She'd tried to call Claire back, with no luck. But the message had her wheels turning.

What did Claire see?

Who?

Considering who it is...

Was it possible she was referring to Abby Collier's killer?

Considering who it is...

Who the hell could she be talking about?

She'd almost called Zander immediately after receiving the voicemail, but considering how things were left off—with the tension between them, and the fact that he'd been called to another murder scene—she decided to wait until morning.

Raven glanced at the clock, again. Six more hours until sunrise. Six more hours of pacing the damn house.

She sipped, savoring the burn of the liquor down her throat.

As Raven turned from the window, a pair of headlights bounced off the walls. She grabbed her gun from the coffee table, turned off the lights and squatted down.

The engine rumbled up to her house and cut off. Her heart pounded as she heard the door slam shut.

Boots up the porch steps, and then...

Knock, knock.

A knot squeezed her throat as her finger slid over the trigger.

Ding, ding.

She crab-walked to the edge of the den and peered into the hall. Thunder rumbled.

The doorknob jiggled.

Oh, my God.

Her cell phone rang. *Shit!* She hit the mute button and looked at the caller ID.

Lieutenant Zander Stone.

She exhaled, pushed off the floor, and opened the door. "Hi."

His hair was wet, his eyes shaded and puffy with exhaustion. Frustrated, irritable, and short-tempered—she could see it all over his face.

"Come in. You're soaking wet."

"Thanks." He stepped inside. Scowling, he asked, "Is it too late?"

"No. Here, let me take your coat. I'll dry it off."

Zander stared at her for a moment, and she could tell that his mind was reeling. With what, she wasn't sure.

He narrowed his eyes. "Why are you still here?"

Raven sighed, shook her head. "I'm not going to get into this with you right now, Zander. This is my house, and I'm not leaving. I've got my gun, and there's no way in hell I'll be able to sleep. No one's going to get past me. Not tonight. Here, give me your coat."

He sighed, as if he literally didn't have the energy to fight with her at the moment, then slipped out of his coat. "Thank you."

"You look like you need a drink."

He hesitated but then nodded.

She led him into the kitchen. "Beer?"

"Beer."

Raven grabbed two beers, popped the tops, and handed him one.

He tipped it up and drank half the bottle in one gulp.

She sipped, leaned against the counter. "Tell me."

His eyes darkened. A moment passed, then he said, "Another one."

Her stomach rolled. "Just like Abby?"

"Just like Abby."

A tingle ran up her spine. "My God, Zander."

He nodded, took another gulp. "Which is why I don't want you staying here tonight. Raven, we can only assume it's the same person. Whoever did this is following you, too, and knows you're snooping around."

Raven glanced out the window at the storm beginning to rage outside. Zander was right.

She looked back at him. "Who was it?"

"A woman named Claire Banks."

The beer slipped from her fingertips and shattered on the floor.

Like a flash, Zander was by her side.

Her mouth dropped open. *"What?"*

"Raven, are you okay?"

She started to speak but couldn't force the words out.

"Raven, what? What's going on?"

She grabbed her cell phone, and with a trembling hand, played the voicemail and handed it to him. His eyes widened as he listened to the message from Claire. He pulled the phone away and looked at the timestamp.

"This was right before she was murdered. What the hell is she talking about?"

Raven took a deep breath, and then told him about the

afternoon rendezvous Claire had with Eric Stevens, and the story of her visit to the salon the next day. She told him about Claire's nervous demeanor, and how Claire had been researching hatchets online. By the time she'd finished, her heart was racing with utter shock.

"Eric Stevens." He said the name slowly, as if trying to remember every encounter he'd ever had with him.

"Do you know him?"

"No, I've only seen him around town a few times. You think he's just a booty call?"

"Possibly."

"Only one way to find out. I'll check his story..." he glanced at the clock. "First thing tomorrow."

She couldn't believe it. Was she last person Claire had contacted before she was murdered? What if she had answered the phone? Would Claire still be alive?

A wave of nausea washed over her. "I need some air." She stepped forward and slipped on a piece of broken glass. *"Ow!"*

Zander swept her off her feet and sat her on the countertop. Blood dripped onto the floor as he lifted her foot.

"Shit."

Raven squeezed her face at the tingling pain. "It's okay. It's nothing."

"It's not nothing. You've got a two-inch piece of glass in your foot."

"Two-inch?"

He nodded. "Might need stitches. You have a first-aid kit?"

"Under the sink."

With his hand firmly on her leg—so she wouldn't fall—Zander kneeled down and pulled the kit from below the sink.

He picked up the tweezers and glanced up at her. "Want your beer for this?"

"Whiskey."

He grinned and grabbed the bottle from the counter.

Raven took a gulp, and so did he, before leaning in and carefully removing the glass from her foot.

"Son of a *bitch*."

"Yeah, it's deep. You okay?"

She nodded as he dabbed the wound with hydrogen peroxide, and then, with surprising gentleness, applied three butterfly stitches.

"Stay here, let me clean this up."

She took another drink of whiskey while he swept up the glass from the floor.

"Zander." Her voice was low and weak with exhaustion. "What are you going to do?"

He stopped, looked at her. "I'm going to find the son of a bitch."

She nodded, looked down, and took a deep breath. Then, she looked up to see him staring at her with an intensity that made her heart skip a beat.

"You need to get some sleep. And I'm not leaving you alone. I'll sleep on the couch."

"*No*. No, Zander, you don't have to..."

"I insist." He leaned the broom against the counter, walked over to her, wrapped his arms around her waist and picked her up as though she weighed ten pounds. Cradled in his arms, he carried her out of the kitchen. She closed her eyes. He smelled of fresh rain, and that indescribable scent of masculinity—the smell of a *man*.

Raven gripped him tighter as he rounded the corner into the bedroom. The warm glow of a night-light spilled out from her bathroom.

Her heart started to pound, her mind started to race.

She wanted him. She wanted him *bad*.

Lightning lit the room, and then, she wasn't sure if it was the whiskey or the adrenaline, but as he leaned her down onto the bed, she reached up, grabbed his collar, and kissed him.

Thunder boomed outside, followed by fireworks exploding in her head as her lips slid over his.

And then–panic. Sheer panic.

Oh, my God, Raven! What the hell are you doing?

She pulled back, her eyes wide with shock—and embarrassment. She'd never been so forward in her life.

Zander's eyes rounded as he looked down at her, apparently in shock, too. And for a moment he just stared at her with an expression she couldn't read.

She wanted to *die*.

In barely a whisper, she said, "I'm sorry, I'm..." But before she could finish the sentence, his lips crushed onto hers.

Butterflies burst in her stomach as he kissed her. He tasted like warm whiskey.

She wrapped her arms around his massive shoulders as he crawled on top of her, kissing her with a forcefulness—a passion—that she had never felt in her life. Her head began to spin, and every insecurity she had escaped her and was replaced with an animalistic need, an uncontrollable lust, for him—for him to be on top of her. Inside of her.

Goosebumps spread over her skin as he slid his hand up her shirt and onto her breast. His finger trailed her nipple, then squeezed. She gripped him tighter as the sensation zinged through her body.

It had been so long. *Too long.*

And she had to have him—*right now.*

Raven pushed up, her eyes locked on his, and ripped off her shirt. She didn't care about her barely B-cups. She didn't care that she was being so forward. She only knew one thing —that she had to have Zander Stone inside of her, immediately. Nothing else in the world mattered at that moment.

He looked down at her breasts, and the fire in his eyes warmed her. She leaned forward and tugged at his shirt.

Shoes were kicked off, the pants were yanked from each other's body. And finally, her panties, and his boxers.

His hands swept over her bare skin and she squirmed underneath him, flushing wet with desire.

She ran her fingers down his back as he kissed her neck. His body was as hard and cut as she'd imagined. It was absolutely perfect. She couldn't believe it—the man she'd fantasized about for two years was here, right now, naked, on top of her.

And they were going to have sex.

As he kissed her ear, her hand slid down his body, bumping over his six-pack, and found his erection. Her breath caught as she wrapped her hand around him and squeezed.

Oh, my God.

He groaned and then answered back. His hand swept down her stomach, between her legs.

Her heart pounded as he slowly rubbed her thighs, teasing her.

She gripped his back, digging her nails into his skin, begging for him to take her.

His fingertips finally found her opening and slowly slid inside. Raven closed her eyes as he glided back and forth.

Kissing her, he pulled his fingers out, sweeping the wet tips over her inner lips. She pressed her hips forward in anticipation of his finger to move up, just a little higher.

And then, it did.

A jolt of electricity shot through her as he glided his finger onto her clit, and began to lightly circle the tiny, swollen bud. Tingles broke out over her skin. Euphoria gripped her. She was completely overcome by the sensation. The warmth began to spread between her legs, and just as she thought she was about to release, he pulled away and positioned himself over her.

Thunder shook the windows.

With his gaze locked on hers, he grabbed her wrists and pinned them above her head. Her heart skipped madly in her chest as she looked back at him, willing to do whatever he told her to. At that moment, he had complete control over her, and she allowed it. She loved it. And it made her absolutely crazy.

She bit her lip as he lowered onto her, found her opening, and plunged into her.

Zander released a low, husky groan as he slowly slid out, then back in. She closed her eyes, savoring the sweet pain, squeezing around his rock-hard cock.

"Raven." A breathy whisper in her ear, followed by a kiss.

She thrust her hips forward as he pushed deeper inside her, slowly at first, and then faster and faster.

His breath picked up, and hers did, too.

Lightning sliced through the sky outside, illuminating the room and the sheen of sweat on his skin.

Her clit tingled, her whole body began to tense.

"Zander."

"Say it again," he demanded.

"Zander."

He thrust deeper, harder, filling her with every inch of him.

"Oh, *Zander*."

The sensation peaked, and as the orgasm ripped through her, he released at the same time.

His heavy body collapsed on top of her, and for a moment, they both lay there, heads spinning, chests heaving.

"That was..."

He looked up with a twinkle in his eye. A small smile crossed his lips—an agreement of what didn't need to be said.

He swept a strand of sweat-soaked hair from her face, and then kissed her. A soft, sweet kiss that had her melting.

And before she could catch her breath, they did it all over again.

And again.

16

$\mathcal{R}$AVEN CLICKED HER windshield wipers on high and squinted to see ahead. The rain poured down from the steep mountain that hugged the road, and then snaked across the narrow lanes, draining off the cliff on the opposite side.

It was a hell of a drive home.

After their wild, mind-blowing sex the evening before, Raven had fallen asleep in Zander's arms, only to wake up in the exact same position, to his beautiful face in the morning. And after a quick rerun, Zander left to pick up where he'd left off the night before—solving two homicides.

On his way out, he'd made Raven promise that she would stay out of the Abby Collier and Claire Banks case, and let him handle it.

Raven had promised, although every inch of her wanted to continue to help him with the investigation. He also made her promise to hold off on further investigating Eric Stevens, until he could confirm that Eric did—or didn't—have anything to do with Claire Banks's murder.

So she'd gone into the office early that morning and

worked her ass off on the other mound of cases she and Dixie had on their plate.

It was just past seven o'clock in the evening, and Raven was running on three hours of sleep and five cups of coffee. She was officially beat.

Her phone rang.

"Raven here."

"Rave, it's Max."

She straightened, suddenly alert. "Hey, Max, what's going on? Any news on the fabric?"

He blew out a breath. "Let's just say, you owe me more than two macchiatos."

"I'll get as many as you want, Max."

"Good. I estimate the fabric had been in that cave for close to two years. Impossible to pull anything from."

"Dammit."

"Well, I *thought* it was impossible, until I found a piece of hair smaller than the tip of a needle."

"Really? Please tell me you were able to get something from it."

"A tip of a *needle*, Raven."

"*Max...*"

He laughed. "Yeah, I got you a name."

Her eyes widened. "Marsha Welch?"

"Nope, that would be too lucky. No, Sal Jenkins. Owns Jenkins Body Shop. Close to your house, actually."

Raven knew exactly where that was—she'd taken her car there for her last oil change.

"*Definitely* not Marsha Welch?" She couldn't hide the disappointment in her voice.

"Unfortunately, no. That case is still cold as ice. Sorry, Rave. Sal was probably just trying to catch a ghost, or spelunking, or something."

"Okay, thanks, Max. You're awesome."

"I know. And I'll look forward to my coffees, and your impeccable organizational skills next week."

She smiled. "You got it."

"Talk soon."

Click.

Raven tossed the phone in the passenger seat and frowned. She was beyond disappointed that the fabric didn't belong to Marsha—which would have been a huge break in the case—but at least Max had gotten a name. Even though it was probably nothing.

Max estimated that the fabric had been in the cave for two years—right around the same time that Marsha Welch's body was found. Coincidence? Maybe. It was a hell of a long shot, but maybe, just maybe, there was some sort of connection.

Maybe.

She peered ahead. As luck would have it, she was less than a quarter mile from the body shop. She got the faintest feeling that she was onto something. Maybe it was just hopefulness, but she felt it.

As she rounded the corner, the body shop came into view, and—*yes!*—the lights were still on.

Raven parked under a tree next to the garage. She turned off the engine, yanked up her hood and got out.

Classic rock blared from the back as she pushed through the side door. The smell of motor oil and stale coffee filled the air.

"Howdy ma'am, what can I do for ya?"

A short, muscular man with salt-and-pepper hair walked into the room, wiping his hands on a towel. He had oil smudged on his face and an armful of questionable looking tattoos. She guessed he was in his mid-forties, and someone who didn't put up with a lot of crap.

"Hi, I'm Raven Cane. I'm looking for Sal Jenkins?"

"Lookin' at him."

She wasn't sure why, but he was nothing like she'd expected. "Do you have a minute to chat?"

He flipped open his appointment book. "I'm booked through this evening, but can get your car in tomorrow afternoon, probably. What kind of problems are you having?"

"Actually this is about something else."

He looked up, curious. "Okay..."

She shifted her weight, realizing she hadn't planned out how to start the conversation.

"Mr. Jenkins—

"Sal."

"Sal. Were you, by chance, hiking around Hatchet Hollow about two years ago? Give or take?"

Just barely, his body tensed. He glanced down, shifted his weight, and looked back up. "I'm not sure. That's a long time ago. I'm sorry, what was your name again?"

"Raven Cane."

"And you're with?" He picked up a paper clip and began bending it in his hands.

"Black Rose Investigations." She needed to ease him. "I'm just researching an old case, and asking anyone who might have been in the area if they remember seeing anything, or anyone, suspicious. That's all."

His eyes darkened. "You're talking about Marsha Welch."

"Yes, I am."

He looked down again and his cheeks began to flush. Every instinct in her heightened—this guy knew something.

Tiny beads of sweat formed on his forehead as he looked

up, and this time, she didn't see nerves behind his eyes, she saw anger. Fire.

With his jaw set, he said, "I'm sorry ma'am, I can't help you."

A moment of silence weighed down the room as they stared at each other.

"Sal, is there anything you might have seen or—

He cut her off. "No ma'am." He glanced out the window, nervously, exactly as Claire Banks had done. "I've got to close up now, so if you'll..." He motioned to the door.

She slid her card on the counter, and after a moment, turned and walked to the door. "If you think of anything, please call me, Sal."

As she pushed out the door—

"Miss Cane?"

Her heart skipped a beat. She turned as he walked around the counter, and handed her his card. "Please consider us for your next oil change." He paused, narrowed his eyes. "The number's on the back, Miss Cane." And with that, he turned and left the room.

Raven chewed on her lower lip as she pulled out of the gravel parking lot. What the hell just happened in there? She replayed the short conversation over and over in her head until she got home. The rain was coming down in buckets as she turned off the engine. She plucked her cell phone from the console, and picked up the card Sal had given her. She flipped it over and in messy handwriting were the numbers 932.

932?

She frowned. Didn't he say that he'd written his number on the back? No, he said *the* number is on the back.

What number?

Raven looked up at the rain-streaked windshield, in deep thought.

She looked at the card again.

The number.

What number?

She shook her head and blew out a breath of frustration as she grabbed her bag and pushed out of the car door.

Suddenly, her eyebrows shot up, and she looked at the number again.

Oh, my God.

She grabbed her cell phone and jogged up to the front porch.

"You've reached Lieutenant Zander Stone, please leave a message."

"Zander, hey, it's Raven. Hey, how many numbers does a police badge number have? Do the numbers nine, three, two meaning anything to—

The phone tumbled to the ground as the pain exploded through her jaw.

17

*E*RIC STEVENS CROSSED his arms over his chest and leaned back in the metal chair, clearly not grasping the gravity of the situation. "Yeah, we met in the woods Sunday evening, well, late afternoon, I guess."

"Why the clandestine location?" Although Zander already knew exactly what Eric and Claire had done in the woods—thanks to Raven—he still needed to hear Eric's side of the story.

Eric paused, his gaze shifting to the stark white walls of the interview room. "I don't know."

Zander clenched his jaw. Eric was a cocky son of a bitch and being evasive—a combination that made him want to punch a hole in the wall. He glanced at the clock—seven-ten in the evening. His patience was wearing thin. He narrowed his eyes and leaned forward. "I know you're a busy guy, with the constant ups and downs in the stock market, and all. But Mr. Stevens, so am I, with two dead bodies, and all. So if we could just move this along..." he casually leaned back in his chair. "Because I've got plans with the Coleman brothers in about thirty minutes." He glanced at his watch, then back at Eric. "You don't happen to know them, do you?"

Eric's eyes rounded, and Zander knew he had him. But he wasn't here to arrest Eric for insider trading. He'd leave that investigation to Raven. He was here to figure out if the arrogant bastard had anything to do with the murder of Claire Banks.

Eric dropped his hands into his lap and looked down, his cocky demeanor instantly fading. He cleared his throat. "Alright, look, yeah, I met Claire in the woods, and we hooked up, alright? But I'm telling you, I had nothing to do with her murder, and I don't know who the hell did. She... well, I'm sure you know her reputation. She got around, to say the least. Could've been any guy."

"Were you two in a relationship?"

He snorted. "Hell, no. Just sex. I mean, I'd give her little gifts from time to time, flowers, whatever. But that's it. We weren't exclusive or anything."

"How long had you been hooking up?"

"Ah hell, I don't know. A few months maybe? But I definitely wasn't her only dude, if you know what I mean."

"When was the last time you two spoke?"

He leaned forward. "Yesterday—

"The day she was murdered."

"Yeah, I guess."

"What time?"

"Um, around six o'clock or so, in the evening."

"What was the call about?"

"I asked her to come over, hang out."

"What did she say?"

"She said no, that she was having a bad day and was going to have a girls' night. I asked her what was wrong and she told me that she'd just gotten into an argument with someone earlier in the day. Said the whole world's screwed up or something like that."

Zander picked up his pen. "Did she mention a name?"

"No."

"And you didn't ask?"

"No, man, I'm telling you, we don't get personal into each other's lives like that." He frowned. "Oh, but she did say she wanted to get the hell out of town. Move somewhere else. That she didn't trust anyone around here."

"Did she seem frightened? Scared?"

He cocked his head and glanced up at the ceiling. "Actually, yeah, kinda. She seemed real wired."

"And then what?"

"That was it. We hung up and next thing I know, I hear she was killed."

Zander paused. "Lay out your Monday for me, Eric."

Eric cocked an eyebrow. "I was at the office all day, went to the gym after, then straight home."

The office and gym would be easy enough to verify. "What time did you get home?"

"Ah hell, a little before six. I called her on the way home."

"Okay. After she denied you, what did you do?"

Eric's cheeks began to flush. "I, uh, I called someone else."

"Who?"

"Another girl I am kind of seeing."

What a fucking sleaze-ball. "Name?"

Eric gave him the name of a girl Zander didn't know, and then leaned back in his chair. "There's your ironclad alibi, Lieutenant Stone. That's where you were going with this right? She even stayed the night. Oh, and we purchased a few movies, too, which I'm sure you can verify with the cable company."

Zander paused and took one last shot in the dark. "Eric, do you know if Claire was involved in witchcraft?"

Eric pressed his eyebrows together. "No way, man. No way."

Zander nodded, paused. "Thanks for your time, Eric." He slid his card across the table. "Call me if you think of anything else."

Zander leaned back in his chair, squeezed his eyes shut, and ran his fingers through his hair. He was just beginning to feel the threat of a monster headache.

Immediately after the interview with Eric Stevens, he'd verified Eric's alibi for the evening that Claire was murdered. And just for good measure, he also confirmed that Eric was out of town, on a business trip, the day Abby Collier was murdered.

Eric Stevens was not their killer.

Dammit.

The investigation was going nowhere. And everywhere he turned, he seemed to hit a brick wall.

He needed sleep. He needed food. He needed to clear his head.

He needed to find the son of a bitch that killed Abby Collier and Claire Banks.

It was creeping up on eight o'clock, and he was still at the office, feeling like he couldn't leave until he got a damn break in the case.

Any damn break at all.

Who had Claire argued with the day she was murdered? They'd already received the phone dump from Claire's cell phone, and her only communications that day were with Eric Stevens and her friend, Becca, which meant, she must've had her argument face-to-face.

With *who*?

Zander glanced outside in deep thought, and replayed Claire's voicemail to Raven in his head.

"I can only assume that you came to visit me to discuss what I saw Sunday night. I want to meet... I'm not comfortable discussing this over the phone, considering who it is."

He had absolutely no doubt Claire was talking about the killer—the same person she'd gotten into an argument with earlier in the day. He just had to prove it. What had Claire seen? What did she argue about? And who would make her too fearful to come forward? Someone of a high social status? Someone involved in something nefarious? Someone that had some sort of power—whether it good or bad—he was sure of it.

And whoever that person was, had their sights set on Raven, now.

The thought had his blood boiling.

When he'd awoken next to Raven, things had changed. Everything had changed. His mind was clouded, his brain felt like mush. He'd thought about her all day, a jumbled mix of thoughts that kept his head spinning. He felt surprised that he could feel so strongly about someone so quickly and be completely overcome by an insatiable thirst to be with her again, and again, and again. Also, he felt a surge of protectiveness, to keep her safe. But perhaps above all, he felt fear—fear that the killer would do more than break into her house next time. Fear that he could lose her, and whatever the hell was happening so quickly between them.

He'd texted her more times than he cared to admit

throughout the day, confirming that she was safe in the office—and staying out of his investigation. As far as he knew, she was still working, under the protection of the Knight sisters.

He took a deep breath, and blinked the blurriness from his eyes.

Dammit, he was missing something.

Abby and Claire were killed by the same person. He knew it. But was it really possible that Marsha Welch was too?

He clicked on the file labeled M. Welch, and opened the autopsy report that the department had on record, and then the official autopsy report from the state crime lab, and put them side by side on his monitor.

Moonmilk.

There it was, as clear as day on the state file. Moonmilk had been found on the victim's skin and in her hair, which meant that it was a definite possibility that she'd been killed in Hatchet Hollow.

He looked at the file that the department had on record —there was no mention of moonmilk whatsoever. It was as if it had been erased from the report.

Was it possible that someone had altered the file, to throw off the investigation?

But who?

He picked up the phone.

"Ace, Black Rose Investigations."

"Ace, it's Zander."

"Hey, man. Busy with dead bodies?"

"Swimming in them. Hey, I need some help."

"Anything."

"I have a PDF file that I think was altered, some information was erased. Can you use your creepy computer skills to find out by who?"

"Seriously? I could do that with my eyes closed."

"Fantastic. Do it now."

"Alrighty. What's your IP address?"

Zander rattled off the numbers, and in under thirty seconds, Ace had dialed into his computer.

"Okay, give me a second."

Zander leaned back as he watched Ace open multiple files, and run various codes. A minute ticked by.

And another minute.

"I thought you said you could do this with your eyes closed."

A blank page pulled up on the screen, and the words *Fuck You* slowly typed across it. Zander laughed. "Okay, sorry."

Just then, a login report popped up.

"There you go, princess."

Zander leaned forward. "This is all the people that have edited, or altered, the file?"

"Yep."

"Thanks, man."

"No problem, let me know if you need anything else."
Click.

Zander scrolled through the list of names, all of which were employees of the state crime lab, until...

He raised his eyebrows.

DMalone, 1:32 am, April 10.

Zander frowned. Deena wasn't assigned to Marsha's case. What the hell was she doing reading the file? Or, messing with it?

Nerves tickled his stomach, and he pushed out of his

chair and walked down the hall. He stepped into Deena's office and remembered that it was her day off.

He flicked the light.

It was a freaking mess.

Stacks of papers covered the desk, four empty coffee mugs lined the windowsill, and the trash can was overflowing.

He stepped over to Deena's desk and glanced at the few small framed pictures that sat to the side—each of various exotic beach locations that she'd visited. He rolled his eyes at one where Deena was flexing in a leopard-print bikini. Was that really appropriate for the office? He stared at it for a moment, frowned and leaned forward noticing a gold necklace around Deena's neck—with the letter *E* dangling from it.

E? *Humph.*

He started skimming through the mounds of paperwork when a stack of black and white photos caught his attention. He frowned, flipped through them, and realized they were taken from a street camera. Each photo showed a dark blue truck parked in front of an apartment building, with the license plate ending in XPG—Johnny Campos's plate. The photos confirmed that Johnny was home on the night of Abby's murder, and therefore, had nothing to do with it.

Why the hell hadn't Deena told him?

Just then, Hunter popped his head in.

"Your phone was ringing." He tossed the phone, and Zander caught it mid-air.

"Thanks." He clicked it on—one missed call from Raven. He played the voicemail.

"Zander, hey, it's Raven. Hey, how many numbers does a police badge have..."

He continued to rifle through the papers on Deena's desk as he listened to her voicemail, but then froze.

"Do the numbers nine, three, two mean anything to..."

Nine, three, two.

His gaze landed on Deena's police badge, lying on top of a folder.

932.

As her last word cut off, a loud banging vibrated through the receiver—like a phone tumbling to the ground.

18

———————

RAVEN'S EYES OPENED to total darkness. A wave of nausea swept over her. She squeezed her eyes shut. Her jaw throbbed with pain.

She was soaked in sweat, but she was shivering.

Where the hell was she?

Thud, thud.

Her body bounced up and down.

Another big bump, and her head hit on something.

Ice-cold terror sliced through her veins when she realized she was inside a trunk. The trunk of a car. She was gagged, and her hands and ankles were bound.

Raven's pulse skyrocketed as she tried to make sense of what was happening.

She replayed her last memory.

She was on the phone with Zander's voicemail, and then a flash of movement from the side, followed by a burst of pain, then her world went black.

Holy shit.

How long had she been out? Where was she being taken

to? Who the hell did this? She hadn't seen her attacker's face, only a glimpse of the fist flying toward her.

Her stomach rolled as the realization began to sink in—it was the same person who put the stone on her bed. The same person who had been following her for God knows how long.

The same person who killed Abby Collier and Claire Banks.

Suddenly the car stopped, and the door opened and slammed shut.

She closed her eyes and pretended to still be passed out.

The trunk opened, and two large hands hoisted her into the air. The rain wet her back as she was carried, over the shoulder, by her captor, into the woods.

Raven's eyes darted around the dark landscape. She inhaled to scream—

"Don't even fucking think about it. I'll gut you right here."

She could barely hear the low voice over the rain... but was that a woman's voice? No, it couldn't be.

The minutes dragged on. Her captor's breath became labored.

Where the hell was she?

Suddenly, a familiar smell filled her nose—wet, moldy earth.

Hatchet Hollow.

She was tossed from the shoulder, and her body slammed against the cold cave floor. Pain rocketed through her head as the breath knocked out of her. She gasped for air and blinked, trying to see through the darkness. A cell phone light clicked on.

And then she saw her.

Officer Deena Malone.

932.

Her stomach curdled as she looked into Deena's wild, feral eyes. And as Deena began to wrap her hands around her throat, Raven released a scream that sliced through the night like an animal being skinned alive.

Zander sprinted down the station steps and jumped into his truck. He turned on his cell phone as he squealed out of the parking lot.

"Hunter here."

"Hunter, I need you to go to Deena's house immediately. Hold her there, and look for Raven Cane. Look for her car or any sign of her."

"What the hell's going on?"

Zander fishtailed around a corner, and horns blared around him. He punched the gas. "I think Deena might be our killer."

"*What?*"

"Just go! *Now!*"

He tossed the phone on the passenger seat and gripped the steering wheel. The rain pounded his windshield as he drove dangerously fast on the slick, mountain roads. He turned on his high beams and clenched his jaw.

He couldn't believe it. Deena—one of their own.

And Deena had Raven, he was sure of it. Now, he just had to find her before it was too late.

Panic had his heart feeling like it was about to burst through his chest as he skidded to a stop next to the Red Rock Trail sign.

Zander grabbed his gun and jumped out of the truck. The rain blinded him as he sprinted down the dark trail. He had nothing but his gut instinct guiding him, and it was screaming at him that Deena had taken Raven to the cave, to suffer the same fate as the two other women she'd so brutally assaulted and murdered.

He jogged through the thick brush, jumping over rocks, fallen logs, and puddles. His adrenaline surged as he pressed on, through the ink-black woods, with tunnel vision.

The terrain started to get rockier, and he knew he was close. He listened for any sounds, but could only hear the buzz of the rain around him.

All of a sudden, a spine-tingling scream echoed through the air.

Zander pushed to a sprint and jumped over the large rock that led to Hatchet Hollow, and leapt into the cave.

The dim glow of a cell phone illuminated Deena, hovering over Raven, with her hands around her neck.

Rage overcame him.

He lunged forward and with the strength that only comes from pure, raging adrenaline, he threw Deena off of Raven, and slammed her body into the cold cave wall. Deena pushed off the wall and swung at Zander. Zander dodged the blow, and before Deena could react, he shoved the barrel of his gun into her neck.

"Don't fucking move."

Deena spat blood on the ground as Zander yanked a pair of handcuffs from his belt. As he slapped them around her wrists, he noticed deep scratches down Deena's arms. He had no doubt that those scratches were from Abby and Claire, fighting her as she strangled them to death.

As Deena grumbled and spat, Zander turned and fell to his knees beside Raven's body. "Are you okay?"

Tears ran down her face. "Yes, yes."

Zander leaned down and stroked her head, frantically looking her over. Emotions flooded his system. "I'm going to get you out of here. You're okay. Okay? You're going to be okay."

After cutting her bonds, and tying Deena's ankles together with the rope, Zander swooped down, picked Raven up, and carried her out of Hatchet Hollow.

19

SAL WRAPPED HIS hands around the Styrofoam cup, gazing into the coffee that he hadn't touched, and took a deep breath.

Zander glanced at the two-way mirror, then back at Sal, who was visibly emotional. Emotional to finally be able to tell the story that had been haunting him for two years.

Zander leaned forward as Sal continued, "I was just about to wrap up my hike when I decided to take a detour to my truck. I was tired, you know, from working at the shop all day." He cleared his throat. "I came up on Hatchet Hollow and heard something inside. I thought it was a bear, actually, but... for whatever reason, something drew me to look inside." He looked down, his body tensing. "And that's when I saw it. Deena Malone, strangling Marsha Welch to death."

The room fell silent. Sal's hands began to tremble, and he pulled them down into his lap.

"It's okay, Sal. I know this is tough. Do you want some water, or maybe to take a quick break?"

Sal shook his head. "Hell no, man. I want to get this out.

I want to make sure Deena Malone gets locked away for life."

"Okay, then, keep going."

Sal took a deep breath. "I ran into the cave and asked her what the hell she was doing, and she jumped up, startled, and then shoved a gun between my eyes." He shook his head. "I should've... I should've fought her or something, but to be honest, I was in total shock. She asked if I knew who she was, and I said yes, and she told me that if I ever told anyone about what I saw that day, she'd frame me for Marsha's murder, and make sure I never saw the light of day again. She said she could do that, easily, because she was a cop." His jaw clenched. "The next fucking day, my house was broken into, and I knew... I just *knew* that it was her, taking something to plant in that damn cave. To frame me if I ever came forward."

"The fabric."

"Apparently so."

***

Zander's boots sank into the mud as he walked around Deena Malone's backyard. It had been less than twenty-four hours since he'd arrested Deena, and the house was swarming with law enforcement. He'd called in every resource imaginable to help look for evidence. They'd already found an old, empty bottle of chloroform, which had been recorded stolen from the station two years ago. The same chloroform that had been used to knock out Marsha Welch.

The four inches of rain they'd gotten the night before had done a number on the yard, but Zander was determined to check every inch of Deena's property, so they wouldn't miss a thing.

The late afternoon sun peeked through the grey clouds

that insisted on sticking around. A warm breeze swept past him as he slowly walked to the edge of the property line, scanning every inch of the ground, looking for anything that might help lock Deena up for life.

Just then, Hunter walked up. "Stone, I think you're going to want to see this."

He looked up.

"We found a bloody hatchet in the garage... and a damn shrine of Eric Stevens in her bedroom."

Three hours later, Zander sat across from Chief of Police Mason Moretti and the district attorney, Conroy Donovan.

Stacks of papers covered the desk.

Moretti blew out a breath and leaned forward. "Folks, what we've got here is a psychotic, obsessed woman who can't let go." He looked at Zander. "Is that what you're telling me?"

"Yes."

"Okay, let's recap for Donovan." He took a deep breath. "Let's begin with the Marsha Welch homicide. First, I should say that most of this information was obtained through Deena's personal laptop, through a personal email account, where she communicated frequently. When she ran security for the state capitol building, her phone doubled as a work phone, so she did most of her personal communication via email. All the emails we're going to talk about are included in these papers, but I'll give you the cliffs notes."

Donovan nodded, and Moretti continued, "According to the email account found on Deena's laptop, she and our buddy Eric Stevens met at the capitol building over two years ago, and over the course of the following few months they struck up a relationship—

Zander cut in. "Aside from the shrine we found in her house, there's a picture on her desk where she's wearing the letter *E* around her neck—for Eric. She became totally obsessed with him."

"To say the least. She drove to Devil's Den several times to meet with him. Wrote him love poems, sent him romantic e-cards, pictures—that will forever be burned into my brain." He shivered. "As the long-distance relationship progressed, she surprised him by quitting her job and putting a down payment on a house here in Devil's Den, for them to live in together. She'd already submitted her damn application here at the station. After she told him this, he got freaked the hell out. Big argument."

"Chick's got balls."

"Understatement of the century, man."

Moretti nodded and continued, "So regardless of the argument, she packs up, moves here and per the email chain, on her first night here, they get into another massive fight. Eric goes to a bar where he meets some random chick —but never mentions her name—who he gets drunk with, takes to his truck, and makes out with."

"Who's the chick?"

"Marsha Welch."

"How do you know it was her?"

Zander crossed his arms over his chest. "On a hunch, I went to every damn hole-in-the-wall bar in the area where a lonely guy might go after a fight with his old lady. I looked through the security footage at each bar for the date range of the emails, and bingo—found him and Marsha Welch cozied up at the Demon's Dungeon, right outside of town."

"Damn you're good."

Moretti leaned back. "The next day, he officially breaks it off with Deena. He confesses and dumps her. Said everything was happening too fast. Told her to stay away from him, his apartment, everything. Told her she was just was too intense for him—his words exactly. This was the last email he'd sent her." He picked up the papers, shuffled through them. "To say she was pissed in an understatement. She called him one hundred and three times over the next few days."

"Psycho."

"Yep, and then, thanks to Sal's confession we know that she goes to the trail—possibly had been stalking Marsha at this point—and kills the woman who she blames for the end of she and Eric's relationship. Then alters the autopsy report to throw off the investigation."

Donovan shook his head. "Where the hell is Eric now? Why didn't he feel the need to bring this up two years ago when Marsha was murdered? Did he know Deena killed her?"

"Eric's in interview room one, barely talking at the advisement of his lawyer. He's shocked. Says he didn't know Deena did it. Says he didn't tell us about the hook up with Marsha at the time because he thought it was irrelevant. And honestly, I think he was a little freaked out. Didn't want to be associated with it."

Donovan nodded. "Okay so we've got Sal's eye-witness account, the empty bottle of chloroform, the psycho emails, the security footage, and the proof that Deena altered Marsha's autopsy report to throw you off. This is good."

Moretti nodded. "Now fast-forward two years later to Abby. This is where we go to the phone records. There had been no communication between Deena and Eric since their last email two years ago, until four days ago when

Deena ran into Eric, who was flirting with Abby at the gym, where she works. Deena texted him and went nuts, especially when Eric called her a nut-job and said he was going to ask Abby out."

"Snarky guy."

"Later that day, Eric leaves for a business trip, and Deena goes back to the gym, casually strikes up a conversation with Abby and invites her to go to the trail the next day. We have this on camera."

Donovan leaned forward. "And Abby took the bait."

Zander shook his head. "Bitch punched her, knocked her out, and took her to the cave, where she woke up, fought Deena—scratched her. And thanks to Deena's recent training at the Academy, she knew to cut off Abby's fingers to conceal the evidence."

Just then, Hunter walked in and tossed a handful of black and white photos on the chief's desk. The grainy pictures showed a woman carrying someone through the woods. "I just got these. They're still-shots from one of my buddy's game cameras. That's Deena, with Abby Collier over her shoulder, less than two yards from Hatchet Hollow, obviously walking that way." He pointed to the timestamp at the bottom of the photo. "On the exact day and time she was estimated to be murdered."

Zander picked up the pictures, passed them around the room.

Donovan flipped through them. "There's your smoking gun, guys."

The room fell silent for a moment. In deep thought, Moretti said, "Is there any connection here to the witchcraft Abby had been studying?"

Zander shook his head. "Not that I can tell. Seems she just decided to take a different path in life."

Moretti frowned. "Bad luck comes to those who study the darkness, boys. I don't believe that's a coincidence." He looked at Zander. "What about the book she mentioned in her note? The *Great Shadow Book of Secrets*?"

"It's not in her house, her car, or anywhere we looked. Assuming that it exists, of course."

"Do we know who was converting her?"

"No, sir."

"Someone did, no doubt about it. I know her family, and I knew her when she was little. No way in hell she just woke up and decided to become a witch, Zander. Someone got in her head." Pause. "We need to figure out who the hell it was."

"Yes, sir."

The chief shifted in his chair. "Still no leads on Marden Balik's whereabouts?"

Zander clenched his jaw. "No. Nothing at all."

"Find her. Figure out if she's the one spreading propaganda. And Zander, if that damn curse-book does exist, find it, too. It needs to be burned to ashes."

"Yes, sir."

Donovan scooted to the edge of his seat. "Okay, so what about Claire Banks?"

"Claire was an unfortunate causality of this love triangle. She uncovered the truth, and died for it." Zander shuffled through the papers and pointed to a highlighted group of texts. "We don't think Deena knew about Claire and Eric's secret fling. Apparently, Deena and Claire were friendly. Claire texted Deena last week about getting some security cameras for her shop. The night after Deena killed Abby, she invited Claire over to look at her equipment." He paused. "The *thing* Claire saw that she referred to in the voicemail to Raven was the damn bloody hatchet in the garage. And after she heard about Abby's murder the next day, she put two and two together and confronted Deena about it. That was the argument that Eric Stevens told us about. The argument Claire had that day, was with Deena."

Moretti nodded. "And then Claire was scared out of her mind, and eventually called Raven Cane, to confess."

"But it was too late. Deena had been watching her, plotting her take-down."

"As she had been watching Raven, too, when she started poking around the case."

Moretti shook his head. "I fucking can't believe it. Marsha, Abby, and Claire."

"And Raven, if Zander hadn't been there."

The chief stood. "Let's go talk to our girl."

Raven glanced out the front window as a pair of headlights cut through the darkness.

She smiled.

She wiped her hands on her apron, took one glance in the mirror, and after smoothing her hair, padded down the hall. She opened the front door just as Zander stepped onto the porch.

Butterflies fluttered in her stomach.

"Hi."

"Hi."

He stepped inside, looked down at her for a moment with a soft smile, and then pulled her to him, wrapping his big arms around her.

Raven inhaled, smelling the scent that she had become so obsessed with over the last few days—the scent of Zander Stone.

Zander kissed the top of her forehead, then pulled away and lightly lifted her chin. He gritted his teeth as he looked at the bruising along her jawline. "How are you feeling?"

She pulled his hand away and smiled. "Fine. I promise."

His face dropped. He grabbed and squeezed her hand. "Raven, I—

"Zander, seriously, I'm fine. Please, I don't want to talk about my damn chin. It's just some bruising. It's fine." She stepped in for another hug.

"Okay." He squeezed her and took a deep breath. "What smells so amazing?"

She smiled as he looked toward the kitchen. "Dinner."

Excitement flashed in his eyes. "Dinner sounds amazing."

"You don't even know what it is. Maybe I made you mountain oysters or something."

He slid out of his coat and hung it up. "Sweetheart, I'm so hungry right now, I'd eat cow brain."

She grabbed his hand and led him down the hall. "It's almost ready. Come on, I'll get you a drink first."

She pulled two beers from the fridge and handed him one.

"Thanks." He sipped, leaned against the counter, and she could see the exhaustion in his eyes. It had been a full day since the horrific incident in the cave, and Zander had been working nonstop.

Raven frowned and leaned against the counter across from him. "Tell me. How did it go?"

He took a deep breath. "She confessed."

"*What?*"

"She would've been stupid not to, with all the evidence we've got mounted against her. She's going to plead guilty, to avoid the death penalty."

Raven set the beer on the counter and walked over to him. "Regardless, she'll be locked up for life, right?"

He nodded, and pulled her to him. He squeezed her tightly, lightly rocking back and forth. After a moment, he pulled away and looked into her eyes, his face full of intensity.

He tucked a piece of hair behind her ear. "Be with me, Raven."

Her heart skipped a beat.

He continued, "Be mine, be my woman. I want you as my own. Only you." He softly ran the tip of his finger down her cheek. "I want to be with you, Raven."

Tears filled her eyes. "I'm yours, Zander. I have been since the second I laid eyes on you."

He smiled and exhaled as if he hadn't been sure what her response was going to be. He lightly grabbed her face. "I'm going to make sure nothing ever happens to you again, Raven. You'll always be safe with me."

And with that promise, Zander kissed her, swept her off her feet and carried her to the bedroom.

20

HE SUN SHONE down from a sapphire blue sky as a warm breeze swept over her skin. Spring was in the air. Raven tilted her head up and smiled, letting the warmth of the light wash over her.

"Another beer?"

She nodded and handed Ace her empty bottle.

"What am I, your maid?"

From across the table, Roxy laughed as the other women of Black Rose—Dixie, Harley, Scar and Fiona—pulled up chairs.

It was a beautiful, abnormally warm afternoon, and because of that, Roxy had decided to move their team meeting outside, onto the patio. And because of Raven's near-death experience a few days earlier, she'd decided to serve drinks along with it.

To help with team morale, of course.

Roxy, the unofficial leader, mother, and indisputable toughest PI of Black Rose Investigations passed out a stack of papers. "First and foremost, congratulations to Raven for successfully closing her first case."

Raven smiled as she received cheers from around the table. "Thanks."

Raven had arrived at work early that morning, to twenty-six voicemails, one of which was an anonymous tip that Eric Stevens was on his way to see the Coleman brothers for a secret meeting on the outskirts of town. She pretended that she didn't recognize the voice of Harold Schumer, the owner of Eric's firm. And after four hours of staking out the scene, she'd finally, *finally*, gotten the money shot—the picture of Eric Stevens accepting a stack of cash in return for divulging stock market secrets. Not only was it her first case successfully closed, it also gave Zander a reason to arrest him, which made the entire town of Devil's Den happy.

Roxy leaned forward. "Okay gang, we'll get to updates on everyone's current cases in just a minute, but a little housekeeping first. We've got the bug guy coming tomorrow morning to spray for shit, so please," she cut a look at Dixie, who was notoriously messy, "please clean up your offices before then."

Ace took a sip of his beer. "Hopefully he won't find a dead black cat anywhere."

A moment of silence slid by as the group exchanged wary glances.

Raven cleared her throat and leaned forward. "How many is that this week?"

"Four."

"Four dead, black cats on our doorstep."

"Righto." Ace tipped up his beer. "Here's to Krestel, and the curse she's placed over Black Rose Investigations." He winked at Dixie. "Thanks, Dix."

Dixie rolled her eyes. "We don't really know it's her, Ace. Could be any one of our pissed off clients, or some bored high school kids trying to spook us."

Roxy nodded. "That's right. The legend of Krestel, and the fact that we uncovered her, has been the constant talk of the town lately. You can't go anywhere without hearing about it. So yeah, it could be anyone, playing a sick, twisted, practical joke." She looked at Raven. "Anything new with the *Great Shadow Book of Secrets*? Did Zander find it?"

"No. Makes me think that Abby was in the early stages of converting. Maybe the book hadn't come her way yet."

Roxy nodded, her eyes darkening. "If the book does exist, we need to get it, girls. Destroy it."

Ace sipped his beer. "I bet y'all twenty bucks that the book exists. Hell, you can't convince me that she isn't using it on us now. She's known for her epic revenge curses."

"And you can't convince me that Krestel really exists, Ace." Roxy inhaled and shook her head, as if to shake away the bad energy. "Anyway, back to business. Next, we've got—

Just then, the force of the blast propelled the team into the air, and tumbling off the patio. Tables and chairs crashed around them. Shattered glass shot like bullets past their faces as fire exploded through the house windows, sending smoke barreling into the air.

And as the team of Black Rose Investigations opened their eyes and blinked away the disorientation, they looked up at the sky just as the black smoke swirled into the letter *K*.

∼

Grab the next book in the series, TOMB'S TALE, today!

ABOUT THE AUTHOR

Amanda McKinney is the Amazon Charts bestselling and multi-award-winning author of more than thirty romance and thriller novels. Her books have received over fifteen literary awards and nominations, including the prestigious *Daphne du Maurier Award for Excellence*, and have been included in lists such as *POPSUGAR's 12 Best Romance Books*, and featured on the *Today Show*.

Sign up for Amanda's newsletter for new releases, promos, personal stories, and plenty of fun extras!

www.amandamckinneyauthor.com

Made in the USA
Monee, IL
07 July 2026